BUCHAREST UNBOUND

RICHARD WAKE

MANOR AND STATE, LLC

Copyright © 2024 by Manor and State, LLC

All rights reserved.

No part of this book may be reproduced in any form or by any electronic or mechanical means, including information storage and retrieval systems, without written permission from the author, except for the use of brief quotations in a book review.

This is a work of fiction. All incidents and dialogue, and all characters with the exception of some well-known historical figures, are products of the author's imagination and are not to be construed as real. Where real-life historical figures appear, the situations, incidents, and dialogues concerning those persons are entirely fictional and are not intended to depict actual events or to change the entirely fictional nature of the work. In all other respects, any resemblance to actual persons, living or dead, events, or locales is entirely coincidental.

SIGN UP FOR MY READING GROUP AND RECEIVE A FREE NOVELLA!

I'd love to have you join my on my writing journey. In addition to receiving my newsletter, which contains news about my upcoming books, you'll also receive a FREE novella. Its title is *Ominous Austria*, and it is a prequel to my first series.

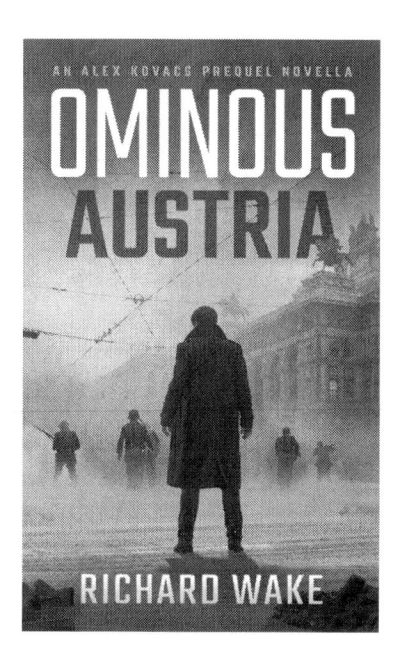

The main character, Alex Kovacs, is an everyman who is presented with an opportunity to make a difference on the eve of the Nazis' takeover of Austria. But what can one man do? It is the question that hangs over the entire series, taking Alex from prewar Austria to the Cold War, from Vienna, to Switzerland, to France, and to Eastern Europe.

To receive *Ominous Austria*, as well as the newsletter, click here:

https://dl.bookfunnel.com/g6ifz027t7

PART I

1

The American Bar was, as ever, tiny, relatively uncrowded, and devoid of women. It was where we always began the night when we were in our 20s — after the first war, before the second, young and dumb and hopeful. The Manhattans were strong at the American back then, and the conversation tended toward the women we intended pursuing at the next stop of the evening. Leon called the placed "the starting blocks," the place where the pursuit would begin with some alcoholic preparation. Then, as now.

"Does she have a name?" I said.

"Frieda," Leon said.

"Age?"

"A gentleman doesn't ask."

"Which lets you out. Age?"

"Twenty-nine," Leon said.

"Jesus Christ."

"It's within the bounds of acceptability."

"Yeah, if you're a statutory rapist."

"Hey, hey, I break no laws — never have."

"Except the laws of decency."

"You're just jealous."

"Whatever happened to half your age plus seven being the lower limit?"

"That's for amateurs," Leon said. "And, you know, she has friends."

I snorted. "You do know that we both turn 50 this year."

"Just a number," he said.

"A big fucking round number."

"Listen, Mr. Alex Kovacs, the number is only as big and as round as you let it be."

I snorted again. This had always been the way of our relationship — Leon having copious amounts of sex, me having less; Leon trying to encourage me to have more, me putting him off. He slowed down a little during the war in Paris, when we were in the Resistance, but it was temporary.

"A sexual blip" is what Leon called that time when he talked about it, which wasn't often. But when he did, the words were always accompanied by a slap to his temple. In his mind, that short stretch of his life was like when the radio lost the signal for a second, and you fixed it with a sharp rap on the side of the cabinet.

"You ever think about it?" I said.

"About what?"

"Paris. Leaving Paris. Coming back here."

"Back home, you mean?"

"Here. Home. Whatever."

At the end of the war, Leon and I were in Paris and without a clue about the future. Neither of us had lived in our hometown, in Vienna, since 1938. It had been seven years away from home but, given the cavalcade of events in those seven years, it might as well have been 70. It was me who suggested we come back home. My reasoning then was simple enough. The Resistance years had been brutal. We had both done things that were best buried in the recesses of our memories — but true burial would be impossible, at least for me, if every time I turned a corner to buy a baguette, I was reminded of some or other atrocity that had been committed by the Nazis in Paris or by me.

The way I explained it back then was, "A soldier, after the war, goes home — and home isn't the battlefield where he did his fighting." Leon ultimately agreed, and we made our way back to Vienna. What we found was a divided city, a wrecked city in many ways — physically by the bombing, but wrecked in other ways as well.

Leon, though, resumed living. He got another newspaper job and worked in his spare time on what he hoped would be his magnum opus, a history of the French Resistance. We had lived enough of it ourselves, after all — in Lyon and Limoges, in fetid alleys and barren countryside, and in Paris most of all — that he could easily sell his personal story. But he wanted it to be more than that, and he pecked away at the book when he could.

Like I said, he resumed living. Me, not so much. I had plenty of money in the bank but not much else — no career to speak of, no friends other than Leon. And I couldn't settle. I was paralyzed by my restlessness, if that made any sense. And I was guided by — consumed by, really — the idea that I really was only good at one thing anymore: espionage. And if my work for the Gehlen Organization after the war took me to places where I made a difference — and it did — that objective good was always being weighed against the moral compromises along the way. When you routinely have a conversation with yourself where you justify the murder of one man because of some nebulous, greater good, well, that is one fucked-up way to live your life.

But it was even more than that. The temporary, tattered relationships. And the necessary rootlessness. And the inability to make anything remotely resembling a true and lasting connection with another human being other than Leon. And the odd comfort I felt in being isolated. And that other conversation with myself about how it wasn't possible to get close to anyone so why even try? Like I said, fucked up.

I would come home to Vienna between missions and hate it. Even as my feelings about the Gehlen Organization grew darker, I just couldn't come home and embrace the light — and a normal life.

"I mean, seriously, Alex. You don't want to go back to Paris, do you?" Leon said.

"Not really, but—"

"What about all that business of living on the battlefield?"

"I didn't say I wanted to go back. It's just the idea does pop up now and then. I just can't get comfortable in Vienna. I'm not sure why."

"Let me fix you up with one of Frieda's friends."

"Sex isn't the answer."

"Maybe not the only answer, but a start," Leon said.

With that he began to tell me a story about the one before Frieda, and the things she did with various vegetables and household utensils, when the door of the American opened behind my back.

Leon paused his story at the chapter on turkey basters and looked over my shoulder.

"What?" I said.

"Grim death just arrived."

2

Fritz Ritter was my boss at the Gehlen Organization but he was more than that. Back when, he had been an old running buddy of my late Uncle Otto. Fritz was a traveling inspector for the Abwehr, German army intelligence. Otto, like me, was a traveling salesman who serviced the clients of the family magnesite mine. They met in the 1920s when they found themselves on adjacent barstools — and when they discovered similar proclivities when it came to the pursuit of unattached women on the road.

In the late 1930s, Fritz found himself working against the Nazis from within the Abwehr. When Otto was killed because he inadvertently found himself caught between Fritz and a persistently nosy Gestapo captain, and I attempted to pursue the truth, Fritz ended up using me but also protecting me. That has always been our relationship, using and protecting.

I felt a bond, through everything. Leon, meanwhile, thought I was blind. From his point of view, "Fritz will use you until you're useless, and he'll protect you until he can't. Either way, you end up fucked in the end."

Anyway, Fritz sat down and ordered a round. The pleasantries consisted of two words: "Alex... Leon." Two words and two nods, and then he started talking about something in Bucharest. I stopped him and gestured in Leon's direction with my thumb.

"Not a problem," Fritz said. "We checked him out a long time ago. The guy I had do it, he came back and said you two might as well be fucking married. And then the guy said, 'They're different but really the same. Two assholes in a pod.'"

"No higher compliment," Leon said. And then Fritz began telling his story. It involved a botched operation in Bucharest, one in which a Gehlen operative had been killed. It also was, at its foundation, a demonstration of the fundamental premise of the Gehlen Organization's existence. That is, Gehlen — a former Nazi intelligence officer — provided the United States with the personnel and contacts that it lacked behind Churchill's Iron Curtain, and the United States provided Gehlen with the cash it needed to exist and to grow.

"So, an American op?" I said.

Fritz nodded.

"But our guy was the one who got whacked?"

Another nod.

"And the Americans?"

"Warming their asses by the fire, and blaming everyone else who was within reach, and reminding us — as punctuation after every fucking sentence — how much their money meant to our survival."

"Sounds like Americans," Leon said.

"Said the espionage expert," Fritz said.

"I've dealt with American men. I've fucked American women. They always make it about the money in the end."

Fritz raised his glass in salute.

"So, what exactly happened?" I said.

"Exactly isn't part of this conversation, unfortunately. Fog of war and all that. It was supposed to be a pretty simple thing. The group—"

"Wait, wait, back up. What group?"

Fritz gave Leon a look. It was the "this is really secret, asshole" look. Leon's reply was a nod that was appropriately grave. Knowing him, though, it was all a put-on. Leon didn't consider anything to be that grave and hadn't since the end of the war. He had seen grave during his time in the Resistance. This, I'm sure he thought, was just adults playing at adult games, the dead body notwithstanding.

"The group is an anti-Communist, I don't know, squadron," Fritz said. "A dozen people, maybe. Homegrown opposition, based in Bucharest. The Americans got a guy in there from Budapest, somehow, and he helped them, shall we say, gather together a group of the like-minded. He helped form them, and he funded them, but he was out of his depth and had the humility to admit it — that, or his bosses admitted it for him. That's where we came in."

"So, we sent a guy," I said.

"We didn't have to send him — he was in Bucharest already. It's the Gehlen special talent. We have somebody in every eastern shithole you can think of. Usually several somebodies."

Fritz went on to sketch out what he knew, acknowledging that what he knew was almost entirely what the Americans had told Gehlen. There were six Bulgarians who had slipped over the border to Hungary when the Communists took over, and who wanted to go back to Sofia and form their own anti-Communist group. It shouldn't have been that difficult. The Gehlen guy knew the area, and the six had slipped over the border once themselves, so as Fritz said, "Not a cinch, but hardly a long shot."

"But alone?" I said.

"I know, I know," Fritz said. "Fatal flaw."

"Literally."

"For whatever it's worth, I wouldn't have designed it that way or permitted it if I had been told. But I wasn't told."

"Why not?"

"Bit of a cowboy, our man in Bucharest," Fritz said. "But I had him on a pretty long leash."

"That's a mistake."

"Said the guy who fucking throws away the leash whenever I send him anywhere — throws it away before he checks into his first hotel."

"Fair enough," I said.

"Not to interrupt your reminiscences, but what do these groups do — you know, the one in Bucharest?" Leon said.

"Sabotage, mostly. Blow up fuel depots. Bomb government buildings. Just be a pain in the ass."

"A lethal pain in the ass, no?" Leon said.

"Goes without saying," Fritz said, and then he continued. The place where the border crossing was to take place was near a Romanian town called Pilu. It was about two miles from the border. There was a main road, which everyone involved knew to avoid. Instead, there were dirt tracks — narrow paths, really — the smugglers along the border had been using forever. On one of the paths, there was a dilapidated lean-to where the Gehlen guy sheltered, waiting for the six to cross.

"The information was clear," Fritz said. "He radioed it to me before the mission. The intelligence he was working with said Pilu. The intelligence said the lean-to. But it was a goddamned disaster. I didn't hear from him, his people in Bucharest didn't hear from him, so after a day, they went looking. Our guy was dead in the lean-to — throat cut. The six Bulgarians were all dead about 100 yards away, just on the Romanian side of the border. All shot."

"Christ. So where did the intelligence come from? Did he develop it on his own?"

"It came from the American," Fritz said. "His bosses swear it was legitimate."

"And where did the American get if from?" I said.

Fritz shrugged.

"That's the fog of war part," Fritz said. "I'm reliant on what our American cousins are telling me. We have the dead body and they have a million explanations. That's kind of how it goes when something goes wrong. Truth is, the Americans didn't invent ass-covering. I got to be an Abwehr general, and I have to admit, well, nobody gets to be a general without developing that skill set."

We all took a drink, and then Leon said, "Maybe the Romanians fucked up — wouldn't be the first time."

Fritz listened to that and looked at me. I burst out laughing. So, he looked at Leon again and then at me again.

"It's a long story," Leon said.

"That involves a woman he slept with in Paris before the war. She said she was a Romanian countess."

"Some fucking countess," Leon said.

"The special kind of countess who gives you the crabs," I said.

Fritz burst out laughing and immediately pivoted to a story from about 1930 that involved him, Uncle Otto, two girls from Frankfurt, and a creaky set of bunk beds.

"And the crabs," Fritz said. "Otto got them, not me. I'm pretty sure I didn't shake his hand for a year."

3

Of course, Fritz wanted me to go to Bucharest. Of course, I expressed my skepticism even as I knew all along that I was going, and that the truth was, I was happy to be going. This was the dance, though. There was something about my relationship with Fritz that I demanded it and he tolerated it. And all through the conversation, Leon sat with his arms folded and a wan smile on his face. Occasionally, he shook his head and laughed.

After five minutes of Fritz going through the logistics of me getting there, I said, "But what's the point?"

"To find out the truth," he said.

"The truth about what?"

"About everything."

"That's a little all-encompassing, no? The truth about everything? Maybe you can send Sartre, or Kant."

"Can't send Kant."

"Why not?"

"He doesn't speak the language," Fritz said.

"Neither do I."

"But you're a quick study."

Fritz had been carrying a knapsack when he walked into the bar. He slid it across the table to me, and I opened it. Inside were four phonograph records and a Romanian language textbook.

"It's high school level — should be good enough," Fritz said.

"Good enough for what?"

"For what it's worth, the countess with the crabs taught me a couple of the sex words. I think I remember—" Leon said.

I was born in Czechoslovakia and spoke that still, if infrequently. I had been in Vienna since high school and tended to think and dream in German. My French had become first-rate during the war. My English was good if not excellent. I had bits and pieces of a few other languages, too. I came to it all pretty naturally, kind of like Leon with the sex words.

"There's also the address of a native Romanian speaker in there — he's on our payroll," Fritz said. "Spend two weeks with the records, and then a week of lunches with our guy, and you'll be good to go. The truth is, German is mostly how you'll get by."

"In Romania?" I said.

"Lot of German spoken there, you'll see."

"You seem pretty confident, especially since your ass is going to be warm by the fire here."

"If you'll let me explain your cover story, you'll see."

"In a minute. Seriously, what the fuck am I trying to find out? How the Gehlen guy got killed? What went wrong on one operation? Seems like a waste of time, and an undue risk of your best agent."

"High opinion of yourself, no?"

"Say it, old man."

"One of our best agents, yes," Fritz said.

"Best agent."

"Give it a rest."

"Best."

"Okay, best. Asshole."

"Best asshole — I'll second that," Leon said.

"Really?" I said.

"I'm here for the comic relief."

Fritz went on to explain my cover story and he was right. My Romanian wouldn't need to be much better than rudimentary, and I would be better than that after a couple of weeks of immersion. But, in the end, I kept coming back to the question he was having trouble answering. Why?

"It's not just to find out why our guy was killed," he said. "In fact, that really isn't a priority. It was clearly a fuck-up on a couple of levels, and the guy was a cowboy, and, well, whatever. What we want is for you to take his place, not find out how he died. And what we want most of all is to get a sense of what the Americans might be up to."

It really was the oddest relationship, the one between the Americans and the Gehlen Org. Leon and I had talked about it not that long ago, and he defaulted to sex. As he said, "It's a relationship where the guy is in it for the pussy and the girl is in it for the money. One using the other, and vice versa, and no truth in the transaction."

"You seem pretty disgusted for a guy who's done the exact same thing a hundred times."

"A dozen times, not a hundred," Leon said. "I don't usually have the money it takes to hold up my end of the deal. But you're right. It never ends well."

It was very obvious what was happening, if anyone was paying attention. The Americans were so Commie-phobic that they were willing to lay out the cash for even half-assed intelligence from the East — and Gehlen had enough people in enough places that the work product was generally north of half-assed. And as for Gehlen, well, it was also pretty clear that he was angling to be the head of intelligence in West Germany whenever it was decided by the overlords that West Germany would be allowed to have an intelligence service of its own. The best way to do that, he figured, was to get married to the Americans and to use their money to expand his footprint.

Every operation into which I entered was, from my perspective, viewed through that Gehlen-American prism. And if I was an anti-Communist — well, at least an anti-Soviet — it was usually hard for me to assign a whole lot of nobility to my handiwork. There was always the Gehlen-American prism, and the level of politics above that, the one I would never have a chance of understanding. Gehlen was undoubtedly like those guys in the park who played a half-dozen games of chess simultaneously, and I was the guy who still had to trace with his fingertip where the knight was allowed to move.

"The old man himself wants you to go," Fritz said.

"Really, now? The old man? Is he older than you?"

"Barely. Maybe."

"Herr Gehlen. Well, well. The kindly old Nazi himself."

"On paper, like me," Fritz said.

"Bullshit. You were fighting them in the 1930s."

"I was still in the party."

"You didn't have a choice."

"None of us did, Alex," Fritz said. "You had to be a party member to get promoted in the army. You're being naive if you doubt that. And he's really worked to keep the worst Nazis out of the Org."

"Now who's being naive?" I said. He knew what had happened to me in Estonia. He knew I had almost died, and then I had almost quit — and if I had had any other life, I would have quit.

Fritz took a long drink.

"Look," he said. "Like I said, this is coming from Gehlen himself. I can't quote him directly, wouldn't be proper, but the gist of it was, 'We might need their money to eat, but that doesn't make them fucking competent. Only fucking wealthy. And when you carry your brains in your wallet, it means you're thinking out of your ass.'"

"A poet, our boss," I said.

"Actually, the last part was me," Fritz said. "And, the more I think about it, I'm pretty sure I stole that from your uncle."

4

The lobby of the Athenee Palace was like out of a 1930s movie — all marble and carpets and chandeliers and characters arrayed around the space, none of whom seemed to be exactly as they advertised.

To the right, there was a bejeweled dowager with a helmet of hair that needed attention sitting at a table next to a painted twenty-year-old who, if she wasn't a hooker, had missed her calling. Across the way, there was a middle-aged, well-dressed man — well-dressed if you ignored the shine of his jacket elbows — joining a man of similar age and shine for a coffee. In the back, a thirty-ish-year-old man sat at a table by himself, using his newspaper less for reading and more, it seemed, for camouflage. Flitting among them were three different waiters — well, maybe not flitting; more like shambling with a purposeful disinterest — their trays laden with coffee and water and whatnot.

And then I remembered what Fritz had said, the last thing before I got on the train: "Remember, when you look at the people sitting around the lobby for the first time, it's as likely as not that they all work for the Securitate."

"Reservation for Kramer, Alex Kramer," I said. I handed my

passport across the front desk to a younger man who smiled and welcomed me to what he said was "Bucharest's grandest hotel." He had not yet developed the purposeful disinterest skill yet. It would happen, though. It would just take time. The kid would be sneering at customers as he took their money in months. Maybe weeks.

The kid paged through a ledger and ran his finger down a column of names.

"Yes, Mr. Kramer, I have it here," he said. "An open-ended reservation, correct?"

I nodded.

"We're obviously not going to hold you to it, but we do always ask for an approximate length of stay," he said.

"Two months, give or take."

"Very good, sir. Welcome to the Athenee Palace! My name is Beniamin. Just call me Benny, everyone does."

The truth was, I had no idea how long this was going to take. I was hoping for two months but was prepared for more. Maybe much more.

The cover story that Fritz and the Gehlen people had concocted for me was both simple and complicated. They wanted me to have a legitimate purpose for being in Romania, and access to what Fritz described as "the nest of vipers hanging around the Athenee — because you never know what you can find there." But they also wanted me to have the clandestine half of my existence, the one where I joined the anti-Communist underground group as the Gehlen Org's replacement for the dead guy.

"And we really don't want the left hand to know what the right hand is doing," Fritz said.

"They're both my hands, old man."

"You know what I mean."

I did — and that was the complicated part. But the backstories really would be fairly simple. The underground would know me by my real name, as Alex Kovacs, former Czech spy, former member of the French Resistance, current Gehlen operative parachuted in to take the place of the dead cowboy. At the Athenee, though, I would be Alex Kramer, a man with a mission to do good in a bad world.

I filled out the registration card and slid it back to the kid. He looked at it and said, "Iacobeni? Where's that?"

I told him. Iacobeni was a dot of a town about 180 miles to the northwest of Bucharest. It was a town full of Germans — or rather, immigrants from Germany who arrived in Romania starting in the Middle Ages and continuing on until 1940. They came for all kinds of reasons — economic, religious, political — and found a home in the mountains. The truth was, Transylvania was lousy with Germans, even if most people in the country didn't realize it.

In Iacobeni — population, 8,000-ish — the majority of the inhabitants were German. They spoke German. They were okay enough with the situation when the Nazis were in bed with the Romanian government. After the Nazis, though, things changed. Their German-ness, so long a non-factor, was suddenly a very big factor. And when the Soviets/Communists took over after the war and decided that they needed workers in the motherland to rebuild, well, let's just say the German-speaking pockets of Transylvania were particularly fruitful regions of conscription. It's amazing what you'll volunteer to do when they're pointing a rifle at you.

And, well, Alex Kramer's story was that he — a local merchant — had been introduced to the business end of one of those Soviet rifles and was deported to a labor camp in the Ukraine. After 18 months, he had been released. Now, he had decided to make it his life's work to try to try to rescue as many of his fellow German-speaking Romanians from the camps as possible — or, at the very least, to find out where they were and to give their families at least that much.

The beauty of the Alex Kramer identity was that there was, in fact, an Alex Kramer from Iacobeni who had done time in a Ukrainian labor camp. The Gehlen Organization had rescued the real Alex Kramer and resettled him with a new name and a stake in a new business in Cologne. I was roughly the same age as Alex Kramer, and our looks were vaguely the same. The real Alex Kramer had no wife or children, so there was no complication there. The real Alex Kramer had no living relatives in Iacobeni, in fact, just in case anybody went looking. And on the off chance that I came into contact with anyone who had ever driven through Iacobeni, or eaten a meal in Iacobeni, I had memorized enough background information to fraud my way through a cursory conversation. As it turned out, the Romanian speaker who I practiced with over that week's worth of lunches in Vienna knew enough about the place to tell me that The Stag served a passable schnitzel, and that mini-avalanches on the north approach road were not uncommon in winter, and that a tiny nun called Sister John the Baptist was the principal of the little Catholic school all through the 1920s and 1930s.

So, I could survive on that level. If, on the other hand, a long shot came in and I ran into a former resident of Iacobeni, I was likely sunk if the conversation lasted more than five minutes — but, well, no cover story is ever perfect. Besides, if a spy spent his life worried about long shots, he would never leave his couch.

So, I arrived in Bucharest with a list of Germans from Romania who had been sent to labor camps — real names, a real list. My stated intention was to find them, and my reason for choosing the Athenee Palace if anyone asked was because it was clearly a crossroads where government officials and academics and traveling businessmen and spies ran into each other on a daily basis.

"A suite, yes?" the desk kid said.

I nodded.

"For extended stays, we customarily require two weeks in advance, with weekly payments every Friday thereafter."

He told me the amount, and I pulled a wad of Romanian currency from my wallet. Fritz had told me ahead of time that, by the official exchange rate, the suite would cost about $1.50 a day in American money.

5

After checking in, I changed out of my blue suit and left the hotel dressed in more casual clothing that would not draw much attention in any circumstance. That would be my traveling outfit, a sweater and slacks, the one I would wear when I was moving between one of my identities and the other. But I would need work clothes, crappier clothes, to wear when I was working for the anti-Communist underground group and living in my crappy room in the student district. Thankfully, there was no shortage of places to buy such clothes in Bucharest, new or used. I went with a smattering of both, new and used, but only after paying extra at the consignment shop for pants and a shirt from, as the woman said, "our guaranteed fumigated section."

It wasn't a 15-minute walk from the hotel to the university, most of it on Calea Victoriei, which clearly was the main drag. There were palaces and what looked like an opera house and whatnot closer to the hotel, and then street after street of what passed for high-end shopping in a Communist country after the war. The sidewalk was clogged with people in the middle of the day, window-shopping in stores that were pretty much empty on the inside. I had no idea about the mornings and the evenings, but it would be among my first scouting missions. Easy and reliably anonymous travel between my two beds and my two identities was a key priority.

The apartment was in one of a dozen buildings near the university that had vacancy signs in their front windows. I could have played one off the other and gotten a better deal, but there was no point. The rent in the first one was the equivalent of about $3 a week for a pretty big room on the third floor with a bathroom down the hall, and that seemed fine.

"There's a rule against women in the rooms," said the guy who took my one-week's rent along with a one-week's security deposit.

Pause.

"Not a hard and fast rule," he said.

Pause.

"As long as you're, you know, hard and fast — no overnights," he said.

Leon would like this guy who never cracked a smile. His name was Ion. He handed me bedsheets and a towel and retreated to his place on the first floor. I made the bed and tried out the toilet, which was clean enough, but I was bored after 10 minutes and decided to wander around the university district for a bit before making my initial contact, the one that would be cemented following the exchange of the most absurd code word I had ever been given.

Just walking aimlessly, it hit me how much the area seemed like every other university district I had ever seen — stately old buildings with signs out front like "Faculty of Economics," and crappy rooming houses, and cafés full of young people arguing about whatever, and older people nursing cups of coffee through the afternoon. I stopped in one place and had a piece of cake at about 5 p.m., having been warned by Fritz that no self-respecting Romanian ate dinner before 9:30. Everybody in the place was doing the same thing, eating something sweet. All I could wonder was what time they got to work in the morning and what time they left.

As it turned out, the streets got crowded at about 8, which must have been the end of the workday. A lot of people seemed to stop for one or two before heading home, and that's what I did, too. And if I wasn't the oldest guy in the bar, I was in the older cohort. If I hadn't been dressed in my guaranteed-fumigated shirt, I could have been mistaken for a professor of zoology or something. I liked to think I would be the kind of professor of zoology who was routinely banging coeds after office hours but, well.

One drink in one bar, a second drink in a second bar, a third drink in a third, and then I made my way over to The Dancing Waters, a café on Strada Slanic. My impression from the door and the faded sign out front was that it was one notch above shithole, a typical student kind of place. I opened the door, and saw that the lights were reasonably bright — not too bright but not a cave — and decided it was two notches above. Then I took a step and downgraded it to maybe one-and-half notches above after I felt my feet sticking to the floor.

About half of the tables were occupied, and the pitchers of beer seemed to be of a reasonable size, and the clientele was like the coffee houses — which this was during the day, no doubt. That is, most of the tables in the middle of the room were full of kids alternately arguing and laughing about whatever, and a few of the tables on the periphery were taken by older men nursing one or two through the night.

My instructions were straightforward. I had been given the code word and I was only supposed to use it on the woman behind the counter. If it was a man, I was supposed to come back another day. Woman, man. I could handle that.

Fritz had said the woman, if she was there, would be pretty — and he was not kidding. Behind the counter, half perched on a stool, was a woman in her mid-thirties with blond hair pulled back in a bun. The green apron that she wore, stained with whatever, couldn't hide the curves.

As I stood at the door, surveying, a kid at one of the tables dropped a half-full pitcher on the wood floor. It thudded hard but didn't break, and the woman behind the counter barely looked up from the book she was reading.

"You assholes know where the mop is," she said, and one of the kids got up and opened a closet door next to the cash register and got to work on the cleanup.

I sat down and the woman brought me a small pitcher and a mug. I sat there for a half-hour and took it all in — the growing-drunker kids, the forlorn old men, the rack of newspapers threaded through bamboo poles like in Vienna, newspapers that likely hadn't been touched since lunchtime. The conversations were growing more animated, the laughs louder — especially when the one kid leaned a little too far back in his chair and ended up on his back.

The place smelled of spilled beer and cigarettes. A fog hugged the tin ceiling and it was maybe six inches thick. Laughing and cursing and beer and smoke — there was all of that, and there was the woman with the curves reading the book behind the counter.

A few minutes after I finished my beer, I looked at my watch. Just 9 p.m. Thank God for that piece of cake. The woman put down her book, and walked across the room in her green apron, and threatened the pitcher-spiller with ejection if he dropped a second one. One of the kids made an attempt to grab her ass, and she intercepted his arm and twisted it behind his back in an instant. The kid screamed in pain. His friends howled.

After all of that, she visited my table.

"Another?" she said.

"Do you have any rhinoceros on the menu?" I said.

Stupidest goddamned code word: rhinoceros.

6

She started walking away from the table, and I didn't move. She stopped, turned, and gave me the "well?" face, which was akin to the "you idiot" face, in my experience, when it came from a woman. From a man, the face was translated almost universally as "come on, asshole." With women, though, the difference seemed to be one of familiarity — and if it was subtle, it was still distinct. You had to be intimately acquainted, to have a history — one that tended to involve bedsheets — to get the "you idiot" face. Again, only my experience.

Anyway, I took the hint, stood up, and followed her. The café was kind of L-shaped, if the L was toppled on its side, and she was leading me toward the short leg and specifically to a door at the back of the short leg. She knocked twice, opened the door, and walked back toward the alcoholic maelstrom. I never had a chance to ask her name.

There were five people in the room, four men and one woman. They were all seated around a large round table and they all stopped talking as soon as the door swung open.

"Ah, our German friend," one guy said.

"Austrian," I said.

"Same difference."

He stood up and stuck out his hand. His name was Constantin, and I took him to be the leader based on nothing more than body language and the fact that he took charge of the greetings.

Constantin led me around the table and made the rest of the introductions. First was Valentina, whose face betrayed nothing — nothing, that is, other than an amalgam of hate/dislike/distrust. Constantin introduced her as "my right hand." At that, one of the other guys snorted, "Yeah, the one he wipes his ass with."

Valentina grimaced even harder. Constantin said, "The comedian is Bogdan. The quiet one next to him is Bogdan's brother, Florin. And this one is Jake."

Jake. The American.

After the handshakes, and after they found another glass and poured me a measure of what turned out to be a local rocket fuel called palinca, we settled in. They knew I had been sent to replace the dead Gehlen operative, whose name was Andrei, and the conversation got to the failed mission pretty quickly.

After a toast to Andrei, I shrugged and said, "I didn't know him, obviously. But I guess I've become hardened to it. This life... we all know it can be the cost of doing business, unfortunately."

"How do you know?" This from Jake, the American. I could tell two things form the question. One, that my Romanian accent was already better than his. And, two, that Jake was clearly a Grade A American Asshole.

"Where to start?" I said. The conversation had been anticipated in my advance briefings with Fritz, and we both decided that the truth was the smartest play. It was just easier that way if I didn't have to juggle two completely fictitious backstories. And, as Fritz said, "You'll wow them. I mean, it has been a hell of a life."

Mostly, I stuck to my time in the French Resistance — how it had led me to do things that still kept me up at night, how the knowledge of the evil I was fighting was the only consolation, and how it had cost me my wife and our unborn child in a plane crash while she was fleeing the Gestapo in Lyon.

When we role-played the conversation, Fritz said, "The last part is important."

"About Manon?"

"About Manon and the baby," he said. "Both"

I had long since stopped being paralyzed by the memory, and Fritz knew that. In the years since, well, so much had happened. I had changed, my world had changed, and time had done its work. The thought of Manon and what might have been didn't cost me sleep anymore — well, maybe a couple of nights a year, but only a couple. Oddly, or maybe not so oddly, the worst times were the quietest times, the lowest stress times, the highly alcoholic times. Those were the nights when I would end up thinking more about the baby than about Manon, and feeling shitty about that, and then down-spiraling from there.

"I don't know," I said.

"It will buy you a level of acceptance you can't accomplish any other way, other than saving one of their lives. And we might not have time for that."

"It just seems so, I don't know..."

"Crass?" Fritz said. "Damn right. That's exactly what it is. But Manon was in the business, just like you, and she would understand. Personal loss like that is the ultimate validation in this kind of situation — wife, baby, especially the baby. From the way you describe her, my guess is that she would be furious if you didn't use it."

He had me there. I knew that. Manon was a pro who worked for French intelligence before the war — much more of a pro than I was at the time. She would be pissed if I put myself in even an ounce of jeopardy because I was somehow afraid of defiling her memory.

And so, after I choked out the last bit about Manon and the baby while sitting in that back room of The Dancing Waters — the choking part was legitimate, as it turned out, but I had been prepared to fake it — I took a long sip of the rocket fuel and look around the table. Valentina's expression didn't change. Jake the Asshole's expression didn't change, but he didn't have a reply, either. The other three exhibited a tic of some sort. Bogdan the joker flicked at his nose, and quiet Florin — whose voice I still had not heard — cupped his chin and looked down. Constantin seemed to have been the most affected. If he wasn't wiping a tear away, he was close.

"A German working for the French?" Constantin said.

"Austrian."

"Same difference."

"It was helpful in many situations," I said. And then I went on to tell him about one of the many times Leon and I donned uniforms while in France and pretended to be German soldiers, this time to blow up a Nazi fuel depot outside of Limoges.

"But didn't you ever feel like you were betraying your own..." It was Florin, and he was as soft-spoken as I had imagined.

"Not my people," I said. "We shared a language, but that was it. We didn't share anything else, certainly not the evil."

I looked around the table. The Nazis had been in charge of Romania for much of the war, and it wasn't hard to imagine that, well, if you made a Venn diagram of all of the Nazi sympathizers in Romania in 1940 and all of the anti-Communists in Romania in 1950, well, how many of this bunch would have been inside of both circles?

"It's like this," I said. "I mean, well, what can I tell you? I was on the right side of history. Like I am here."

7

The lobby bar at the Athenee Palace was called the English Bar. It wasn't in the lobby, not exactly — it was in a kind of elevated annex behind the main lobby, up a couple of steps — but the name was perfect. You walked in and, well, it was what I imagined the bar in a London gentleman's club was like. The walls were not painted or papered, but all dark wood that they must have polished regularly. Dark wood, well-dressed men — all men — whispered conversations, and a bartender who could make a proper cocktail. In my case, that was a Manhattan made with rye, not the American bourbon that also was on offer. With my first sip, I found myself smiling and also giggling.

"Something funny?" the bartender said.

"No, no, just so well-made that it reminded me of a happy memory," I said. What it actually reminded me of was how I could drink like myself in the hotel as the fake Alex Kramer but I had to drink that rocket fuel when I was in The Dancing Waters as the real Alex Kovacs.

I sipped the Manhattan, enjoyed it — no, savored it. The initial meeting with the underground group had gone well. The truth was, it didn't really matter either way — they were stuck with me as the Gehlen replacement and I was stuck with them, as we all knew — but a comfortable relationship might lead to a certain level of trust, and a certain level of trust might accelerate my acquisition of knowledge about what the hell was exactly going on, and I was all for speeding up the process and getting the hell home. It was just another aspect of my fucked-up existence — that when I was home in Vienna, I couldn't wait to get back on an assignment, and when I was on an assignment, I couldn't wait to get home.

The bartender slid me a second Manhattan, and I was pretty well convinced that it was human nature to be looking to the next thing, not my fucked-up head. I sipped it, complimented the bartender's skills, and asked his name. As it turned out, Radu had been perfecting his talents behind the same bar since 1929.

"Seen a few things, I would guess," I said.

"You don't have the time or the imagination," he said.

I let him go, not wanting to sound too eager. Fritz had told me this was the way to play it — that is, to confide in the bartender at my earliest opportunity. As Fritz said, "At that fucking place, the Securitate might have the ashtrays bugged for all we know. They certainly have somebody supplying information about comings-and-goings from the taxi stand outside. The hookers in the lobby will be describing you down to your moles and freckles in their morning-after reports. But the bartenders — every last one of them will be on the Securitate payroll. That's a given."

"Why, though?" I said.

"Why what?"

"Why tell the Securitate, by way of the bartender, what I'm doing? I mean, it's kind of illegal, I would say."

"Maybe not so illegal," Fritz said. "I mean, you've seen this before — I remember your reports from Budapest. They might be true believers in the great Communist bullshit, but that doesn't mean they aren't Romanians first — and the names on your list are all Romanians who have been snatched out of their beds. There's dialectical materialism, and then there's grabbing a guy away from his wife and kids and putting him in a labor camp — a Romanian guy with a Romanian wife and kids. So, where will their loyalties be on the question? Split, probably."

"But—"

"And the other part might be more important. True believers, yes, but that doesn't mean they aren't angling to make something under the table. You can be both."

I nodded my head and said, "Yeah, yeah. Thieves wear many different uniforms. But I still don't understand why we're laying it out for them."

"It's human nature," Fritz said. "A new guy comes into the hotel — single man, open-ended reservation — their job is to check you out. Most people, they aren't worth the time to look into their past, but the Securitate, they don't know until they've done the work. So, in the beginning, you're nothing more than work for them, nothing more than a pain in their ass."

"Okay, but—"

"So, you do what you can to make it easier for them. You tell your story to the bartender, just like we practiced it. You give them the roadmap, and their work is easier. The pain in their ass is lessened. They make a phone call, determine that Iacobeni's city hall does, in fact, have Alex Kramer listed on the tax rolls, and they feel better. They digest your story, see you as a do-gooder who probably has some money, and they feel even better. They note that you told your story freely to the bartender, that you were open, that you had nothing to hide, and they feel even better. They drop you down on the priority list. They might note your comings and goings or they might not — but they don't follow you. Not worth it. Bigger priorities elsewhere. Without your backstory established, you would be seen as mysterious and more interesting. Now, not so much."

"Now I'm hurt," I said.

"Right," Fritz said. "And then, in all likelihood, somebody in the Securitate will tell somebody, and that somebody will tell somebody else, and one of the somebodies will have the kind of thieving heart that we're looking to meet up with. But it starts with the bartender."

It wasn't until the third Manhattan that I began to tell him. When he brought me the fourth, I was poring over the list of names and ended up handing it to him to see. He pulled up his stool and sat with me for the fifth — I bought him a drink — and I told him the whole thing. As the story spilled out, the one thing I kept thinking about was when Radu would be telling his Securitate contact. Right after the shift? On the way to work the next afternoon?

While I was sitting there, five Manhattans deep, describing the hell of the work camp in the Ukraine, I even half wiped a tear — but only half, and only for a millisecond. I didn't want to overdo it.

Christ, acting is hard.

8

It was two nights later, and I was again parked at the English Bar when a guy in a dark gray suit sat down at the bar stool next to mine and ordered a martini with two onions.

His first sip approximated my level of bliss, and he looked over at me and said, "Nectar, I say."

I held up my Manhattan and said, "Of the gods."

We were both speaking German, although it took a minute for that to register. I was happy for it, if for no other reason than I could relax a bit. My Romanian required a lot of effort, and it was only decent. A couple of times, I noticed the people around the table at The Dancing Waters slowing down a bit for me. It was only a bit, but it was there. They didn't feel the need to speak the words one at a time in a shout, like talking to a toddler, but they did make the occasional accommodation, and I would just as soon avoid that.

But there was something else, something more important. The guy knew I was a German speaker before he sat down. This was exactly what I had hoped for — an approach.

As it turned out, his name was Cristian Something-or-Other, and he worked in the Romanian treasury department. He described himself initially as a "low-level functionary." In the middle of the second martini, he amended that.

"Let's just say that, while I do push paper for a living, it is the most important paper," Cristian said. "Only the most important."

Whatever that meant. After that is when I explained my fictional predicament — that I was from Iacobeni, and that I had been snatched and sent to a labor camp in the Ukraine, and that I was let go for some unclear reason, and that I wanted to help get others out.

"Iacobeni," Cristian said, and my bowels clenched. I took a sip and tried to relax as he ruminated. The odds that the first guy I talked to would have knowledge of that tiny speck in the mountains were astronomical.

I sipped and he repeated, "Iacobeni." But that was it.

"Ever been?"

"No, no," Cristian said.

"Ever heard of it?"

"No, actually," he said. At which point, I described one or two features, settling on the avalanches on the north approach road for my longest dissertation. He feigned interest until I took out the list of names I was carrying in my breast pocket.

"They're from Iacobeni and other places, as you can see," I said. He took the list and scanned it, names and home towns. It was a legit list that Gehlen had somehow obtained.

"My camp was hell," I said. "They fucking worked a lot of people to death — like, literally to death. The rest of us, we worked all day and then dug the graves of our brothers at night. Just, fuck."

"What can you do, though?" Cristian said.

"I did well in my life," I said. "I have money to, well, ease the, uh, mechanics."

We ordered another drink — my third, his second — and Cristian pawed the list as it lay on the bar between us.

"You're looking to get them out?" he said.

"I have to think the Romanian government would have some say over its citizens."

Cristian snorted.

"Some, maybe," he said. Then he lifted his right hand and held his thumb and index finger about an inch apart.

"The money," I said.

"The money would, shall we say, supplement the influence my government might have."

I nodded.

He nodded.

"As for what you describe as the mechanics," Cristian said. "Perhaps I know someone who could be of assistance. But in order to make the approach, I would need..."

"For you and for him," I said, a statement rather than a question.

"There would be a third level of payment as well, farther down the line," he said.

I nodded. Then I reached into my pocket and removed five $100 bills. I folded them and passed them to Cristian with a handshake. It was probably stupid, paying in advance, but I couldn't risk blowing this approach. Besides, it wasn't like it was my money.

"Two for you, three for your friend," I said. Cristian looked as if he was about to start bargaining, and his lips pursed, and then he stopped himself. By my reckoning, a low level treasury official in Romania didn't make $200 a year — and, if he was smart, he would keep the $300 and offer the $200 to his friend.

"When might I meet your friend?"

"Next week, early," Cristian said. We set a date, and Cristian left, and I had a fourth Manhattan. I was celebrating. Because while I honestly couldn't give half a shit about the names on the list I was carrying around, I needed to make progress on it in order to keep my cover intact, and this was progress.

9

Three days of sleeping intermittently in a cave hidden among the hills outside of Ploesti bore no resemblance to a suite at the Athenee Palace — no clean sheets, no gentle knock on the door when the woman brought the fresh towels, no Manhattan in the English Bar for a nightcap. Very different — not to mention the bats in the cave. Oh, and the bat shit.

It was four of us — me, Jake, Bogdan and Florin. We took shifts with the binoculars, clocking the comings and goings of the Soviet troops guarding the oil refinery. The lookout would call out any movement he spotted, any truck arrivals or departures, any shift change of the guards at the gate, any alteration in the numbers of men near the entrance, or the wells inside, or the massive building where the crude oil was refined into something usable. He would call it out and one of us would record the data in a logbook.

Three days in a cave is not nothing; this just in. The only time we went outside was to use nature's bathroom. It was chilly, but we didn't dare risk a fire to keep us warm. What we were left with were sleeping bags and rocket fuel, the bottles of which were easily the heaviest items we carried in our packs.

We picked a Sunday-Monday-Tuesday stretch in an attempt to get a varied look at the operation. The theory was that Sunday would probably be the quietest day, and that Monday — if it was like most business enterprises — would see a significant ramping up of activity, and that Tuesday would probably be a fair proxy for the rest of the days of the week.

By Monday morning, we were bored beyond reason. The highlight of the previous night's conversation was Bogdan telling the story about how, when he was 16, he was declared the farting champion of his grade in school after a series of elimination bouts, the last of which ended with his opponent crapping himself.

"A technical knockout under the laws of the game," Bogdan said.

"Laws?" I said.

"It was a serious competition. The biggest arguments were always over the rule that allowed for bonus points to be awarded for, and I quote from memory, 'outstanding achievement in audibility and fragrance.'"

"These laws, they were written down?"

"Like I said, it was a true and serious competition."

"Did they give you a trophy?"

"A ribbon, actually," Bogdan said.

"Our family was so proud," Florin said.

"And what exactly did you ever win?"

"Highest average in history and maths at graduation."

"Well, if you're going to get technical about it," Bogdan said.

I was pretty much doubled-over laughing at that point, but managed to catch my breath and ask, "Which one of you is older?"

"Him, 14 months," Florin said.

"God, 14 months. Your poor mother."

"Yeah," Bogdan said. "She still calls 1925 and 1926 'my trial.' Which I never understood. I mean, I was a prince."

A statement he punctuated with a fart.

A fart to which Jake responded, "Fucking animal."

He was one miserable human being, Jake was, and not just because he failed to recognize one of the fundamental human truths — that farts are always funny. He said very little during the three days, other than regularly lobbying to cut short the reconnaissance trip after about a day and a half. Florin was quiet but Jake was surly-quiet, and there was a difference.

The only time he seemed generally interested in a conversation was when the topic turned to what it always turned to in any kind of military/quasi-military situation. I had fought in the first war for Austria-Hungary, back when there was such a thing, and I had been a Resistance fighter in France during the second war, and I had also had occasion to witness more than a few German soldiers in their natural habitat. And it didn't matter if I was freezing in a tent in Caporetto, or sleeping rough in the hills outside Limoges, or on a stakeout in a Paris garret — it was always the same. Within a certain interval, usually minutes, the conversation was reduced to two topics: the incompetence of your superior officers, and sex. I had been involved in such conversations in German, French, and a little bit of English this one time with an American sergeant after the Allies had taken Paris. My operating theory was that, regardless of the language, if I could learn the words for "fucking asshole generals" and "nice, round ass," I would be able to get through a night in a bar with a corporal in any army on the planet.

And so, in the cave, that's where we ended up — except that the two topics were combined, not separate.

Or, as Bogdan said a half-dozen times in the three days, "Of course he's fucking her."

The "he" being Constantin, and the "her" being Valentina.

"I don't know," Florin said.

"You're just winding me up," Bogdan said.

"They might just be soldiers, fighting for a cause. I mean, you're not fucking Jake, are you?"

"The silent asshole speaks," Jake said.

"Okay, you can be the one fucking Bogdan."

"Are you finished with your fantasy, little brother?" Bogdan said. "Christ. You know he's fucking her. It would be unnatural if he wasn't."

"I'm with the farting champion on this one," Jake said. "And I don't like it. I mean, that isn't how this shit is supposed to work. It creates, I don't know, an imbalance. What if we get into a situation, a bad situation, and he has to make a decision about saving one or the other of us. You all know that kind of thing is a possibility, and you'd like to think your leader — the guy you supposedly trusted — would make a calculation based on the group as a whole or the success of the mission. But this guy, this fucking Constantin? You know he's going to save her even if it kills the mission."

"Not to mention, kills us," Bogdan said.

"And that's not right," Jake said. "It's just not right. The leader has to be objective, do what's best for the group and not for his woman."

"I don't know," I said. "Think of poor Bogdan's dilemma. He gets in a spot and who does he save — his little brother or the guy he's fucking?"

Florin burst out laughing, and Bogdan followed quickly. Jake muttered, "Fucking assholes," and went back to the binoculars. And that's pretty much how it went for the three days. When it was over, we had a logbook full of details that told us one thing overall: that the overall troop numbers and the shift changes of the guards at the entrance were precise and consistent. They were so exacting, so perfectly ordered, it was almost like the Germans were still running the operation, which they did during the war. Because, as Jake said, "Ploesti was always the prize, with the Nazis and the Russians, then and now. Ploesti, Ploesti, Ploesti. The rest of Romania was always just a pain in their ass."

"And our job—" Bogdan said.

"Is to increase the pain," Jake said.

10

On the one hand, I had been almost completely honest with Constantin and the rest about my background and my intentions. I used my real name, and offered up a good bit of my real life history, and worked honestly to assist them in their goal — to be enough of a pain in the ass to the Soviets to make their occupation of their country uncomfortable, and maybe worse than that. That was all legitimate.

What they didn't know about, and what I could not tell them about, was the radio.

I couldn't believe how small they had gotten. The one I brought into Romania, sewn into the lining of my coat, was not much bigger than a pack of cigarettes. Every time I marveled when Fritz handed over the latest model, and every time he said something on the order of, "German engineering, brother. The cities might still be bombed to hell, but German technology... Even after everything, still the best in the world."

After the research trip to Ploesti, my job was to radio back the key findings to Fritz. I still had no idea what the mission to Ploesti would be. For all I knew, Constantin had huge ambitions and was hoping to blow up the refinery building. Or, it might have been a less grand plan — something like blowing up a truck on the way out of the front gate or taking out two sets of guards during a shift change. That part would come later — and I might or might not be chosen to be involved. But with the raw data about staffing levels and the timing of changes of the guards, Fritz would have the same basic blueprint that Constantin was given. And if the whole thing went to hell, he would be able to compare it to what the Americans told him and draw his own conclusions. If the plan was adjudged to be flawed, he could blame Constantin. If the plan was sound but things went bad, he could maybe blame the execution of the commandos on the ground. But if there was a discrepancy between my data and what the Americans reported, well, the Gehlen Org would be able to know for sure that the problem was more than just bad luck or the malpractice of a rogue cowboy who had gotten drunk on his own adrenaline. They would know that it was something more nefarious.

Anyway, after three days in the cave, I took a long bath back at the rooming house and was sitting on the bed in my underwear, reaching for the radio hidden between the mattress and the box spring — original, I knew, but what the hell? — when there was a knock on the door. It was Ion, looking for the rent.

"Just a second," I said, reaching for my pants.

"You got somebody in there?"

"Just getting dressed after a bath."

"You sure you're alone?"

I opened the door.

"If I'm ever so lucky, I'll give you a shout and you can watch through the keyhole," I said.

"Appreciate it, but my old knees don't really permit that kind of crouching anymore. I will accept a full recitation of the relevant facts, though."

"A blow by blow, then."

"As it were," Ion said. Leon really would love this guy.

When I got rid of him, I was back to the radio. It came with a little removable earphone that allowed me to hear my dots and dashes, and then to listen to the reply from Fritz. My memory is pretty good, but I was worried that I wouldn't be able to remember everything if the data from Ploesti had been complicated. As it turned out, I lucked out because the Soviets seemed so anal about keeping a consistent staffing schedule. Next time, though, I wasn't sure. I had a tiny camera, and I guess I could have taken pictures of the logbook if it had been complicated, but getting the pictures developed, well, I'd have to steal the stuff I needed from a photographer's studio, and that was a complication I wasn't savoring.

After I sent the data — precisely at 9 p.m., when Fritz or one of his people was supposed to be monitoring the frequency — I waited the required 10 minutes for the reply.

It was one word: "Resend."

My guess was that it wasn't Fritz, because he was as anal as the Soviets about the schedule. It must have been one of his guys, and he must have been late turning on his radio. So, I resent the stuff and waited.

This time, a different word: "Acknowledged."

And, well, you're fucking welcome.

11

The note left for me at the front desk of the Athenee Palace and handed over by the ever-cheerful Benny — "a splendid day, Mr. Kramer" — was from Cristian, the guy from the treasury department whom I had pre-bribed. Well, I assumed it was. He didn't sign it, but he wrote, "I'll be at the English Bar at 7 tonight with the man I expect to become our mutual friend."

For whatever reason — just to throw them off a hair, if nothing else — I went to the bar at 6 and got started. I wanted to watch them walk in, and I wanted them to encounter me before they could do any last-minute conferring. Not that it mattered, really. I was just going through the motions of the Alex Kramer identity that got me into the country. It wasn't as if the amount of the bribe I was going to end up paying the guy was crucial to anything. It wasn't like I was buying a house, after all — and it wasn't my money.

For whatever reason, I had the Manhattan with the American bourbon instead of rye. As Radu dusted off the bottle and poured, I said, "Not much call for it?"

"Not much? None," he said.

"How did you even get it?"

"Beats the hell out of me. But there's a half case of it in the cellar."

"I wonder how long it's been there."

"Before the war, I'm pretty sure," he said. "In the 1930s, this place was a real crossroads. Business people, journalists..."

Then he leaned in and whispered.

"Spies," he said.

I made what I figured to be the appropriate face, one part surprise, one part wonder, one part tell-me-more. He nodded, pleased with himself.

"A den of spies," he said, even more quietly. And then he backed away and returned to the cocktail — which was excellent, for what it was worth.

I was midway through my second when my meeting partners entered. It was only 6:30, and they were surprised to see me, and maybe just the slightest bit uncomfortable. Good.

Introductions were made, except only my name was spoken out loud. Through their first drink, I mostly just repeated what I had told Cristian the last time. I pulled out the same list from the same breast pocket, and the new guy read it slowly, scanning with the assist of his finger. At one point, he pulled over one of the small candles on the bar to help him see better. He really gave it a long, uncomfortable look.

"Another?" I said, catching Radu's eye. At that point, Cristian made his excuses, leaving me with the other guy.

He got right down to the money, naming a figure. I made a face and said "phew," and then, "I don't know."

"The number is the number," he said.

I paused, then agreed.

"Dollars or Swiss francs?"

"You assume I don't want Romanian—?"

"Dollar or francs?"

"Swiss francs," he said, adding a huge grin for punctuation.

"And for that, I get..."

"Twenty names at least from your list, released and delivered."

"Twenty-five."

"Pretty steep. I won't know until I can do a bit more research..."

I was pretty sure that he had already done his research, and knew that whatever he was going to have to pay to get the prisoners released was less than half of what I would be paying. Maybe less than a third.

I paused, sipped. The grin for punctuation told me all I had needed to know. He was locked in. I could have asked for 30 names.

"Okay, 25 names," he said. We agreed that when he had the 25 identified, I would hand over the Swiss francs. I had thought about asking for it to be cash on delivery, but that made no sense. He would need the money up front to pay his bribes down the line. I was just going to have to trust him.

"There's one thing, though," he said.

"What?"

"This makes no sense to me. I mean, what's in it for you?"

It was always the hole in my story, the part that didn't ring true on its face. Fritz told me it was the problem — that is, that Alex Kramer's motives were too good to be true, that the incentives didn't line up with human reality. The story we embroidered was better but still imperfect — but it was the best we could come up with. And, after a deep breath and a long sip, I began to tell it.

"What's in it for me?" I said, repeating the question once, then a second time. "It's a little complicated, but here goes. My father, well, he wasn't the best of men — I'll just put it like that. There are people in Iacobeni who would tell you that he was a cold, thieving bastard, but I'll leave it where I did. Not the best of men."

The guy seemed fascinated, for what it was worth. If nothing else, I had hit the proper tone.

"He made his money through property purchases and sales — real estate transactions," I said. "What he did — what he specialized in — was swooping in and buying distressed properties when people could no longer afford to pay the taxes. He had his whole spiel — before the government takes it from you for failure to pay back taxes, I'll buy it and you'll get something. And what they got was a pittance — and they needed to find a new place to live besides. They had worked and saved for a lifetime, and they were left with pocket change.

"Anyway, he did this all through the time after the first war, the 1920s and early 1930s. He owned half the goddamned town, it seemed like, which meant that half the goddamned town hated him. But he was smart, I have to admit that. And in the 1930s, he began to sense the winds blowing and began to sell off the properties. He was getting three, four, five times what he paid for them — a hell of a return in the space of a decade or so. And then he converted the money — to gold and to Swiss francs — and he sat on it while the world went to shit, and then the Nazis came. And then the old prick dropped dead."

My companion was now rapt. Beyond rapt if there was such a thing. His mouth seemed to be stuck just a little bit open.

"I can't believe I called him 'the old prick,'" I said, mumbling almost to myself before recovering my voice. Christ, acting is hard.

"But, well, I got everything — the gold, the Swiss francs, the remaining couple of properties. And I rode it out, and survived the war, and then I got arrested and sent to the work camp in the Ukraine, and then I managed to buy my way out."

He looked surprised, the first change of expression since I had started talking.

"Yeah, I lied earlier about not knowing why they released me," I said. "It's embarrassing enough to have done it, but to have to explain to people..."

I stopped, took a drink. Fritz and I had actually practiced the pause when we were working on the story.

"Anyway, I don't know," I said. "You're asking me what I get out of it, out of spending my father's money to help people from Iacobeni? What do I get out of it?"

Another pause. Another drink.

As practiced.

"What do I get?" I said. "I don't know. It sounds corny — I'll admit that — but maybe, just maybe, I get my family's name back."

I nodded at Radu, and he brought me another Manhattan. Fourth? Fifth?

It didn't matter. The guy bought the story. Fritz would have been proud.

I let him leave ahead of me with a copy of the list of names. I was nursing my last one when, not five minutes later, a woman sat down next to me.

12

She, too, spoke to me in German without a prior introduction — which, well, I found to be interesting, even in my Manhattan-induced state.

Her name was Sofia Popescu. She was in her late thirties and pretty in that athletic/weather-beaten way, like a farmer's wife used to long days in the sun. Which she was. At least, that's what she said she was. I couldn't shake the notion that the Securitate found me so fascinating that they had decided that they needed to know more — and to insert a woman into my life, so to speak.

"From Resita," she said, when I asked her.

"Iacobeni."

"I know," she said. I didn't reply, seeing as how I had never heard of Resita and didn't know if it was the next town over from Iacobeni, or in the next county, or nowhere near. Silence was my only play.

"I looked on a map," she said. "Nearly 200 miles, best as I could tell. You ever hear of Resita? Because I had never heard of Iacobeni."

I exhaled — hopefully, not noticeably — and proceeded to tell her about Alex Kramer's hometown. I again settled on the avalanches closing the north approach road as my go-to bona fides. She replied by saying that her town and mine were probably pretty similar, and how most of the people spoke German most of the time. She finished with a story about the little Christmas village that the people of Resita put up every year.

"Little Dresden," she called it.

"Shame about that."

"About what?"

"About the real Dresden," I said, and Sofia nodded and took a sip. Then she said, "Little Dresden will always be my Dresden."

Eventually, she got around to telling me the story of the Soviet soldiers coming into Resita and rounding up all of the men over the age of 17, tossing them onto the back of three open-top trucks and driving off.

"One minute, you're living your life, getting ready for the harvest, and the next..." she said.

"Me and the girls..." she said.

"How old?"

"Eight and six."

"Where are they now?"

"With my mother — she lives with us," Sofia said. "I need him back. I got in about 25 percent of the harvest — wheat. We can't live on that. We can't make our payments on that. The vultures are already circling. We've been offered, well, such a small amount..."

I thought about the fictional story about my fictional father, the Iacobeni vulture, and decided to keep it to myself. That was also when I decided that I believed Sofia, and that she hadn't been sent by the Securitate to suck the real story out of me, so to speak.

"What have you done so far?" I said, and she told me the story of going to the labor ministry building.

"It's forced labor, so, I don't know," she said. "And they shuffled me from desk to desk for the better part of yesterday afternoon. The men were nice enough, but they all kind of shrugged. What was pretty obvious was that they had no information about the prisoners or the camps, and they didn't know where to find the information, and they had no intention of trying to find it. Like I said, nice enough, sympathetic enough — but nothing."

The labor ministry was likely full of bureaucrats who did nothing but rearrange the paperwork and punch out every day at the prescribed time. If there was a list, it was in a bigger, darker place — the foreign ministry, say, or the Securitate. That undoubtedly was where my unnamed helper was doing his mining.

"Look, I have money," she said. She looked down, and at that point, I realized why she had been clutching her handbag the entire time, not even resting it in her lap.

"It's not a lot, but it's all we had saved," she said. "It's probably two months of payments on the farm and the equipment and the seed for next year and the rest. But I don't know what else to do. I didn't know, that is, until I heard about you."

At that point, I gave her the abbreviated version of Alex Kramer's story, and then I reached into my pocket and produced the list of names I carried around.

"Give me that pencil," I said, and Sofia reached over to the cash register and snatched one of the pencils from the cup sitting next to the stack of order sheets. I asked her to repeat her husband's named, and I added it to the bottom of the list. Mikhal Popescu.

"Look, there are no guarantees here," I said. "And my people are going to take priority if there's a choice that has to be made — I'm just being honest here. But, well..."

"How much?" she said, reaching into the handbag.

"No, no."

"But I must..."

"What you must do is not get your hopes up," I said. "I'm kind of flying blind here, and I'm not sure how this is going to work out. And it's going to take, I don't know, at least a few days before I have some answers. Probably a week."

I was guessing, but the look on my man's face when we agreed on the Swiss francs suggested that this would be a priority. A week. Not much more.

"Let me at least buy you a drink," she said, and she paid for my Manhattan and for her drink as well. Despite my admonition, her hopes were indeed raised and her smile was suddenly radiant. She gathered her things, got up to leave and kissed me on the cheek.

"One thing," I said.

"What?"

"Well, how did you know?"

"Know what?"

"Know that I was involved in finding people from the camps. Know that I might be able to help you."

Sofia looked down toward the end of the bar, where Radu was washing a few glasses in a sink full of soapy water.

13

The back room at The Dancing Waters was, if nothing else, a haven from the layer of smoke that hugged the ceiling in the main part of the café. None of the members of our merry little troupe of anti-Communist commandos smoked. The odds of this were somewhere between long and astronomical, but I wasn't complaining.

The mission to Ploesti had been set the previous night. I wasn't going, and I wasn't happy about it. If I told myself the truth, it wasn't just because I wouldn't have eyes on the operation and wouldn't be able to report back to Fritz with my firsthand observations. I was pissed because they thought my skills were inadequate.

"I fucking blew up Nazi rail cars, for Christ's sake," I said.

"Not the same thing," Constantin said.

"They don't go boom the same way as they did in 1943?"

"Different explosive, different fuses, different everything."

"Same boom, though. You think I'm too stupid to learn?"

"You're not going," Constantin said.

So, for all of those reasons, I was drinking more of the rocket fuel than I should have been, drunk and pouting. Still, I figured there might be something to learn from the meeting and the interactions, so I tried to pay attention through my increasingly fuzzy lenses.

The mission was simple enough: overpower the three guards at the front gate, hijack the jeep that was always parked outside the guards' shack, drive the 200 yards to the refinery building, and set some charges along the foundation to the left of the main entrance. I mean, like I couldn't blow up a refinery building? Fuck.

There would be four men on the mission: Constantin, Bogdan, Florin, and another American I met that night, Peter. Jake the asshole wasn't going, either. Again, the excuse was a lack of proper explosives training. Peter, their boom-boom maestro, was in and Jake and I were out — but while I pouted, Jake was borderline giddy.

The back room was smoke-free, like I said, but drenched in testosterone. I had been there before and knew what it felt like — the adrenaline building, the exhortations and the alcohol and the brotherhood and the rest. It almost made you hard sometimes, when you were a part of it.

But I was on the outside looking in. And if Jake was giddy and I was morose, the third person not making the trip, Valentina, was playing the role of buzzkill to perfection.

Bogdan was standing and toasting everyone and seemed about ready to rip off his shirt, storm through the door of the back room, and either hug or start a fight with whomever he first encountered in the main room of the café.

That's when Valentina said, "Put it back in your pants, little boy."

"The fuck?"

"It's a military mission, not a goddamned football match," she said. "So everybody needs to calm the hell down and get back to the details."

"We've been through this," Peter said.

"Once more," Valentina said.

"For fuck's sake, woman," Bogdan said.

"Enough, all of you," Constantin said. "Valentina's right."

So, one more time, they went through the details. That was pretty much where I checked out mentally. At the first hint that the meeting was wrapping up, I bolted for the door — and I was halfway across the café when I heard someone calling my name.

I turned. It was the woman who was perched on the stool behind the counter.

"One more," she said.

"I don't know. I'm pretty well shot in the ass already."

"Turn around."

Which I did.

"Your ass looks fine to me."

"Likewise."

"You can't see mine from there."

"I remember from the last time," I said.

Her name was Sabina. She brought a small pitcher and two glasses and pointed to an empty table in the corner. The café was quiet — one table of placidly intoxicated students, one old man in the opposite corner reading a newspaper.

"So, your friends?" Sabina said.

"Still in there. Be done in a minute."

She nodded.

"And you know exactly what?" I said.

"Enough."

She paused, took a sip.

"Enough to be dangerous."

"But not a part of the, uh, group?"

"Officially, no," she said. "Not a part, not exactly. Adjacent, though. Adjacent and, well, supportive."

"Which could still get you into trouble if the wrong people found out."

Another nod, another sip.

And then Sabina said, "The way I figure it, you need things like this in your life — at least, I need things like this — to get my heart started in the morning. I mean, how else do you know if you're alive?"

We finished the beers and chatted some more, mostly making fun of the nearly comatose table of students working their way through two last pitchers.

"You think they can even walk?" I said.

"They'll fucking walk when I tell them to."

"I don't know. I mean, look."

Of the five of them, two of them had their heads down on the table, lifting them only for their next sip. The other three were slumped back in their chairs. One had his eyes closed.

"The redheaded kid, he's like a bull," Sabina said, pointing at one of the kids whose eyes were open. "I kick his ass, he kicks their asses, and out they go — and if they all piss themselves on the sidewalk, well, whatever happens on the other side of the front door is somebody else's problem."

Other than the initial bit of flirtation, there wasn't any more sexual tension between us — at least I didn't feel any. Then again, I wasn't feeling much of anything at that point. Mostly, when I thought back on it, what I remembered was that last question she asked.

How else do you know if you're alive?

14

Cismigiu was the name of the big park in the middle of Bucharest — or, at least, what I thought was the middle. I hadn't seen a map and I wasn't sure, but it seemed like the middle to me. It seemed very big to me. Again, I hadn't seen a map, but what felt like a long walk to me one day barely touched the fringes of the place. Anyway, if the designer was going for "urban oasis" as his blueprint, he hit the mark. I found that once I got 50 feet inside the grounds, I was taken — mentally more than physically — to a different place. Warmer, somehow. Calmer.

There was a lake in the middle of the park — again, what I thought was the middle. Based on the even contours, I was pretty sure that it was man-made, but no matter. Sitting there on the bench, feeling the cool breeze off of the water, it felt real enough.

It was getting toward evening, and I felt the breeze and closed my eyes and let my mind wander. My dual missions in Romania were going just fine, all things considered. The only hiccup so far had been my exclusion from the mission to bomb the refinery building in Ploesti — but that was hardly a fatal flaw. On the one hand, my first-hand, eyes-on observation of events would have been valuable. On the other hand, if the thing went tits-up, the reliability of the narrators who were on the trip could perhaps be tested against each other. If there were discrepancies, well, there was something there that might be worth having.

I opened my eyes for a second and looked out at the lake. There was a rowboat easing past. It held two kids, a boy and a girl, no older than 20. The boy was laid down in the back of the boat, and the girl was next to him with her head on his chest. The boy held a bottle of something, and the two of them shared sips. They were too far away for me to hear what they were talking about. Only her laughter, high pitched, dented the silence.

I closed my eyes again. The real downside of my exclusion from the Ploesti sabotage was the chance that it would delay the end of my trip. The business with the men in the work camps was moving along just fine, and that was good. But if it moved a lot faster than my underground work, there could be a problem. If I were to pay enough bribes and get my whole list of names released, my quote-unquoted legitimate reason for being in Bucharest would be done. At that point, Alex Kramer would be expected to head back to Iacobeni and the avalanches that closed the north approach road, God help him. At that point, would the ladies and gentlemen of the Securitate begin paying more attention? And if they did, what would that mean for Alex Kovacs, anti-Communist commando, who had experienced a reconnaissance trip but who still hadn't seen his sabotage group in action?

I heard a man yelling and opened my eyes. It was the guy who rented out the paddle boats from a small shack at the far end of the lake. He was standing on the bank, yelling and waving at a boat that contained three boys, none of whom seemed older than 15. One of the kids was standing on the one end of the boat, trying to balance, but the boat was rocking precariously, and the man was screaming for the kid to get down, and the three of them were laughing uproariously. Finally, the kid got down — and then, the three of them all began shoveling handfuls of lake water onto each other and laughing even louder.

I closed my eyes again and imagined the kids in the boat were Leon, Henry and I, and that it was about 1915 and we were on the Danube. We had done plenty of shit like that. Fucking Henry. It was in Zurich, where we had been relocated by Czech intelligence after the Anschluss. It was in Zurich, where Henry's father had been killed by the Nazis while helping me with the radio on one of my first missions. Henry had never forgiven me, as if the old man hadn't made his own choices, and Leon had been a kind of collateral damage even though he'd had nothing to do with it. Fucking Henry. I counted on my fingers. More than 10 years now.

I heard one of the boys yell, "Look!" I opened my eyes and saw the lights must have just been turned on, maybe by the old man in the shack, maybe on a timer. But they added a glow to the whole place at twilight, a different atmosphere. Softer. Nicer. But when I closed my eyes, and saw Leon and Henry and I in the paddle boat again, drenched to the skin and angling toward a boat containing three girls who were laughing at us and clearly interested in a drenching of their own.

First, I thought, did that even happen? Then, all I could think about was cutting the trip short and heading home to Vienna. But home to what?

I walked down along the bank of the lake, and then over the wooden bridge that spanned a narrow neck of water. I wandered down one of the dozens of trails, caught a whiff of a sweet flowering bush, snatched the handkerchief out of my pocket and let loose with the kind of theatrical sneeze that often produced uproarious laughter when timed correctly in a movie.

It was then, as I refolded the handkerchief, that I noticed that the shabby-looking man in the light gray jacket whom I saw when I first entered the park was, indeed, following me.

15

The light gray jacket followed me out of the park and all the way on my walk to the bar near the university, the bar with the sign that said "BAR" over the front door. I didn't try to lose him, and my shadow didn't go out of his way to avoid being seen. I had experienced this surveillance thing from both sides, and I knew all of the tricks, and I could tell that the light gray jacket was employing none of them — starting with his attire. Light gray was a lot more memorable than something darker, for instance.

I walked into the bar, ordered a beer, sat at a corner table with my back against the wall, and watched the door. Two minutes, five minutes, 10 minutes — but the light gray jacket didn't follow me. My guess was that he worked for the Securitate, and that he was going off shift, and that he might or might not be replaced. They must have decided that I was worth a quick gander after all — and while this wasn't ideal, it wasn't entirely unexpected, either. No reason to panic. Just a reason to keep my antennae up — and that's always a good thing. As Fritz liked to say, "Complacent agents tend to end up as dead agents. Cause, effect."

I was ordering a second beer when Jake the asshole walked into the bar. I saw him immediately, and he saw me, and I couldn't tell which one of us was more disappointed. Anyway, he got his own beer and sat down at my table.

"'Sup?" Jake said.

I raised my glass.

"Well, we have that in common," he said.

In my previous life — or, more accurately, about three previous lives ago — I had been a traveling sales rep for my family's magnesite mine. What that meant was that I could bore you to tears with facts about the use of magnesite as the lining for blast furnaces in steel mills, or I could arrange for whores of any shape, size or predilection for the mill owner after we signed the new sales contract. Or anything in between. Conversation with people I despised had always been part of the job description, and I was wondering if I might be out of practice. But, as it turned out, I could even carry a long conversation with Jake the American asshole.

It's all about being a good listener and observer. And as soon as I noticed the slightly dismissive snarl when Jake mentioned our Romanian hosts, my work was done. All I had to say was, "The fucking food..." With those three words, like I said, my work was done — and the thing was, they were the absolute truth because the fucking food in that country was terrible.

"Afterbirth on a plate — but that isn't the half of it," Jake said, and then he was off on an anti-Romanian tangent that managed to denigrate the food, the water, the air quality, the architecture, the education level of our compatriots in the anti-Communist cell — even the quality of the women. I just nodded along, even while suddenly being unable to get Sabina out of my head.

"Have you heard the one about, well, what's the difference between a Hungarian and a Romanian?"

"Beats me," I said.

"Both will happily sell their grandmothers, but the Romanian won't deliver," Jake said.

I half laughed politely. The comedian was undeterred.

"You've heard of King Carol, right?"

"Assume I have."

"Jesus Christ," he said. "Okay, King Carol the first. He arrived in Romania in 1866. He was a young German prince, and he was being given the country to take over."

"Lovely gift. Did they tie a bow around it?"

"Whatever," Jake said. "They threw him a big party when he showed up, a big banquet. And, well, the new King Carol lost his wallet at the banquet. There was another prince there, Prince Cuza — I think he was the one throwing the party — and he announced to the group, all of the people at the banquet, that they would extinguish all of the candles. But it would only be for three minutes. After that, they would light the candles again, and Prince Cuza said he expected the stolen wallet to be on a silver platter in the center of the table when he did. That was it — three minutes of darkness and no questions asked."

"I've had sex like that."

"Shut up and let me finish," Jake said. "It's a good joke because there are two punch lines. Depending on who's telling it, well, after they relit the candles in this room full of fucking Romanians, either a) the platter was gone, or b) six wallets were there."

I liked that one. I liked it a lot. Jake was still an American asshole but, as it turned out, he could tell a story. And I was still in mid-guffaw when a guy walked into the bar — staggered more than walked, actually. Jake saw him at the same time I did.

"You know him?" he said.

"I don't know anybody."

"Ever been here before?"

"Nope."

The guy was kind of catatonic — staring and not speaking. But the man behind the bar seemed to know him and handed him a beer without being asked. The catatonic guy sat at a table in the corner, and downed the beer in two, and then a waiter brought him another beer without him asking.

"Just the two, always just the two," Jake said.

"Who pays?"

"Nobody. On the house."

"Really?"

"He's their official charity."

Jake didn't know the guy's name but he knew the guy's story — or, rather, the highlights. He explained that the guy was local, Romanian, an anti-Communist just like Bogdan, Florin and the rest of the people in their crew. And, one day, the Securitate knocked on the door of his apartment and hauled him out by the ankles.

"And then what happened?"

"What happened? Pitesti happened," Jake said.

"And what's that? Pitesti?"

"Jesus Christ, don't you fucking know anything?"

"Just tell me, asshole," I said.

Jake went on to explain that Pitesti was a big Romanian prison, "the crown jewel of the entire — and entirely cruel — fucking system." It was a system, he said, where actual brainwashing was practiced on political prisoners. I asked him how it worked, and Jake replied with a wave of his hand.

"Fuck knows," he said. "But brainwashing, it's a real thing — and that poor fool is Exhibit A. Some people think it's bullshit, just designed as a scary rumor by the Securitate to frighten people, but it's real. I mean, just look at him. They let him go when they were done with him, and now he just wanders around."

Right around then, the guy finished his second beer, stood up, and kind of staggered back toward the door. He hadn't been in the bar for 10 minutes.

"Just the two, always just the two," Jake said, half speaking and half muttering to himself.

"And where does he go now?"

"Beats the shit out of me. You see him on the street sometimes, just wandering. I assume he has a place to live. And his clothes, I mean, they're clean enough. Somebody must be taking care of him on the other end, but I have no idea who."

We both drank for a minute in silence, and then Jake said, "People don't think it's real. Well, fuck. It's like there's nothing in his head anymore. Nothing there. No one home. An empty fucking coconut."

16

The path up to Metropolitan Hill was long and gentle, not really steep at all. It was an easy walk from the Athenee Palace, and when you got to the top, there was a huge plateau littered with massive stone buildings. One, I was told, hosted the Chamber of Deputies. Others were old army barracks and monks' cells and whatnot. The centerpiece, though, was the orthodox cathedral — so it was church and stated married on a vast plain. On Sunday night, though, the politicians were nowhere to be seen and the only praying was done at a small chapel off to the side of the cathedral — small but ornate, walls covered in gold bric-a-brac and frescoes of saints and the like. During the service, the men stood on one side of the center line and the women on the other, and the priest sang/chanted a lot, and the people blessed themselves a lot in that backwards way that the orthodox did it. Or, rather, backwards from my perspective. They likely would say the same thing about me — that is, if I ever blessed myself.

I was early, sitting on one of the benches outside but able to peer into the service and see Constantin, standing and kneeling and blessing himself along with the rest. There weren't two dozen people inside, but he was one of them. If The Dancing Waters was the most-used meeting site, the benches outside of the chapel on Sunday evenings were second. At least, that's what Bogdan said. Rather, sneered.

He arrived next with Florin, then Jake, then Valentina, then the other American, Peter, the explosives expert. We sat around, waiting for the service to end. When it did, and the people streamed out, Constantin spotted us and headed over to the benches.

"Finally," Bogdan said. "Did he throw in a couple of extra hymns this week for good measure?"

"Shut up, when I'm in there praying, I'm saving your sorry asses in more ways than one," Constantin said. He was smiling.

The mission to Ploesti had taken place on Friday night, and this was the debriefing session for the group. I knew it had gone well, mostly because Bogdan had already told me, "Fucking piece of cake." But I didn't know the details, and I needed the details.

What I got from Constantin — he did all of the talking — was pretty much a minute-by-minute account of what had happened. The change of guard shifts occurred exactly as their surveillance had predicted, and the ability of the group to overtake them also had gone as expected.

"How many dead?" I said.

"All of them," Constantin said.

I shrugged and he continued, "If you expected anything less, I don't think you were paying attention."

With that, he continued. The vehicle that was expected to be at the guard shack was indeed there. The single guard outside of the refinery building was, in Constantin's words, "Eliminated with prejudice."

For some reason, I looked at Valentina at just that moment. I must have winced involuntarily at Constantin's phraseology, and the look on her face in reply was a pair of stared daggers. Cold bitch, that one.

Next came the explosives review. Peter was there to set four charges in the space of two minutes, Constantin said, and he managed to set them in 95 seconds.

"The only good news," Constantin said.

"Listen—" Peter said.

"No, you listen. You're the expert. Four charges, two minutes. In my mind the expectation is you set four charges, you get four explosions."

"Well..." I said.

"Well, what?" Constantin said.

"I've done this before, and I've been around the block — even if you think it was ancient history. And, well, there's a lot that can go wrong in that short amount of time. In my experience, three out of four is a realistic expectation. Four out of four, that's a dream. That's not reality."

I couldn't believe I was defending Peter, who I didn't know and whose presence I resented. I did it almost as a reflex, for whatever reason, probably because I saw myself as a card-carrying member of the Fraternity of Men who Blow Things Up. Anyway, I regretted the words almost as soon as I'd said them.

Constantin smiled and waited.

"You finished?" he said.

I said nothing.

"Four out of four is unrealistic — fair enough," Constantin said. "Three out of four is a more realistic expectation, a fairer way to look at the outcome. That's what you're saying?"

We locked eyes.

"Well, how the fuck is one out of four, Mr. Reasonable? How is that? Good try, old chap? Better luck next time, fella?"

I desperately wanted to look at Peter but managed to stay locked on Constantin's eyes.

"One out of fucking four," he said. "One!"

"So, what was the damage?"

"Blew off a corner of the building, but that was about it. A big mess but no big fire. No series of explosions afterward. If they aren't up and running again in two or three days, I'll be shocked."

I still couldn't look at Peter, but I sneaked a peek at Bogdan. I interpreted the look he gave me as, "Screw it. The plan worked." And he was right. The intelligence collection had been solid, and the plan had been reasonable. It was just the execution of the last bit that turned a complete triumph into a minor success — and, well, that kind of thing happened all the time in the business of undercover sabotage.

Constantin returned to a clinical recitation of the end — how they piled into the vehicle, and drove out through the front gate slaloming around the dead guards' bodies, and parked it about a mile down the road. From there, it was back through the hills, and then splitting up for the return to Bucharest.

Constantin asked if there were any questions, and nobody had any. He finished with a move that surprised me, given his disdainful tone during the previous few minutes. He leaned over and offered a pat on the shoulder for Peter. It was almost fatherly, even if Peter wasn't five years younger than Constantin.

I walked back with Florin and Bogdan. Florin, speaking for the first time, said, "You should have come."

"Peter actually pissed himself a little," Bogdan said.

"And he couldn't catch his breath, like," Florin said.

I shrugged. We walked back down the gentle slope, back into the center of the city. When it came time to split up, Bogdan said, "I think Constantin might have underestimated the damage. It was a pretty loud boom. The refinery might be out of commission for a week, which isn't nothing. And the dead guards — I'd say we definitely got their attention. And, well, the intelligence was perfect. The guards, the shift change, all of that. Clockwork. Goddamned clockwork."

I shrugged again and thought about how to radio the information to Fritz in as short a form as I could manage. Because while I had never seen a radio detection truck in Bucharest like the ones I had seen the Nazis use during the war, well, I had no idea what the Securitate might have up its sleeve. I knew how much smaller the radios had gotten in the years since — Christ, lugging around the ones from the Resistance would leave you with a sore arm for days — and maybe the detection gizmos had shrunk, too. I had to assume that was the case and that speed of transmission still mattered.

It was only later when I realized that a perfect plan, one that only failed in the explosive execution, got me no closer to figuring out the problem with the group and the reason for my mission.

PART II

17

After being shadowed on my walk that night from Cismigiu Park, I was particularly attentive whenever I was in the Athenee Palace — well, as attentive as I could manage after an hour or two on one of the stools in the English Bar. Radu had become like an old buddy in my weeks at the hotel, and his cocktails were becoming the kinds of cocktails he undoubtedly poured for his good friends. That is, I was now becoming drunk after two Manhattans and knee-walking drunk about midway through the fourth.

Which is where I was when my still-unnamed intermediary with the people who could spring Romanian men from the Ukrainian labor camps sat down next to me.

I nodded a greeting and simultaneously sneaked a peek over his shoulder. No one had followed him through the entrance. The guy ordered a drink and I felt for the envelope stuffed with Swiss francs that I had carried into the bar every night for the last three nights.

I peeked again. No one. The truth was, I had not spotted even a hint of a tail other than that one night. And even if the denizens of the lobby, the hookers and the old professor-types, all kept any eye on me when I passed through from the elevators near the front to the English Bar in the back, well, so what? As for Radu, well, of course he was working for the Securitate in some fashion. But, so what? I mean, those fucking Manhattans...

Another sip.

"Well," I said.

"Well what?"

"You first."

The guy nodded, took another sip just to piss me off with a further delay of a few seconds, and then reached into his breast pocket for his own envelope. He slid it across to me, took another sip, stood up and said, "Gotta pee."

I removed the sheet of paper from the envelope and scanned it. It was a list of names and camp locations. I took out my original list and compared them. About 30 percent of my names were on his handwritten list, but not Mikhal Popescu. Of course, Mikhal Popescu had only been added to my list after my guy was gone from the bar that night.

"So, what do you think?" he said after returning from the toilet.

"Well, it's a little light."

"You're kidding me, right?"

"It's less than half the list."

"You do realize what you're asking for, right?" he said. "We're not picking up a bunch of kids for an after-school outing to the country. We're going into a Soviet labor camp and paying off enough people to get them to release a bunch of, well, almost political prisoners. Less than half the list? I mean, for fuck's sake."

It was my turn to take a long sip and piss him off with my silence. I knew that he was right but I also knew that this was still a negotiation — and that if I didn't at least play the game, it would come off as suspicious.

"For the amount we agreed on, I need 10 more," I said.

"Three."

"Seven."

"Five."

Another sip.

"Okay, five more," I said.

Another sip.

"One other thing," I said. "No, two other things."

My worry all along had not really been with the mechanics of the transaction. Bribery was bribery, after all, and there wasn't a whole lot of mystery to the process. It could all blow up in the end, but there really wasn't anything I could do about that. And if there was no honor among thieves, well, I still had to trust the thief who was sitting on the next barstool. I didn't have a choice.

No, my concern was about what they were going to tell the men who were being sprung from the camps. The Alex Kramer/rotten father/saving the family name story was plausible enough, and I had practiced it with Fritz before the mission and told it well, but there was no way to know if it would withstand the scrutiny of people who actually knew the real Alex Kramer.

And if the thread unspooled, well...

My concern was the timing. It would likely take weeks to get the men out of the camps. Ideally, I would be out of Bucharest by then and back home in Vienna. The problem was, I had really learned nothing from that first mission to Ploesti. This was going to take more time.

But, well, whatever. I took out the envelope, opened it, thumbed the stack of Swiss francs and removed a few of them, maybe 10 percent of the total.

"More than enough to get you started, more than fair for what we've agreed on," I said. "You'll get the rest when I get the other five names."

My man began to object but thought better of it. He

snatched the envelope from my hand and stuffed it into his pocket.

"Last thing," I said. Then, I reached over, grabbed one of Radu's little pencils from the cup next to the cash register, and handed it to him.

"Write down this name," I said, and he did. Mikhal Popescu.

"Find him and I'll double the amount," I said.

"Double what you just stuffed into your pocket?"

"No, double the whole thing," I said. "If you find him and bring him back alive, double."

When I thought about it the next morning, I knew that it had been the Manhattans talking.

18

Our first date was the next night. It wasn't a date-date, just a walk around Cismigiu Park. It had been Sabina's suggestion. She said she was in cafés far too much during the week to see another meal out as a treat.

"And I checked, and the movies are shit, so, the park," she said.

When I walked to the park, I made sure to check if I had been tailed — but I was certain I was clean. If you had crayoned the route I had taken on a map, it would have resembled a line drawn by a drunken five-year-old in a rage. There was no way I was being followed — I was as positive as I could be. As far as I knew, it had still only been the one time.

Sabina was already in the park when I got there, sitting by herself. I was carrying a bottle of wine when we met and exchanged chaste kisses on the cheek. She saw the bottle and said, "Forget something?"

"Hardly," I said, and then I produced a corkscrew from my jacket pocket, whipping it out like a magician revealing the hidden ace of spades.

"I mean glasses."

"I figured we could just share from the bottle."

"A real romantic," she said.

We walked past the place where they rented the paddle boats and then away from the water, down a path I had not yet explored on my previous visits. After a couple of minutes, we reached a small round clearing where a series of busts were set in a circle around the perimeter.

"The writers' rotunda," she called it.

We walked from bust to bust, each riding a pedestal, and I didn't recognize any of the names. Writers, she said. I felt stupid but also a bit defensive. I mean, what was I supposed to have done? It wasn't as if you could walk into a bookstore in Vienna and find the works of Mihai Eminescu in translation.

We walked around and looked at the dead men's heads. The heads of the dead men I had never read. Head, dead, read.

"You don't have to pretend," she said.

"Pretend what?"

"That you know what the hell you're looking at."

"I didn't realize I was pretending. I didn't say anything."

"Your face did," she said.

She made her way to each of the busts, one after another, and stopped and seemed to lose herself in thought — but only for two or three seconds. About halfway around, though, she stopped in front of one of the busts for a long interval. Ion Luca Caragiale.

"Ring a bell?" she said.

I shook my head.

"Not even a little?"

Another shake.

"Very famous — though, truth be told, I only know one of his works. It was called *A Lost Letter*. They taught it in school back when I was in school. These days, these people, I have no idea if they still teach it."

I asked her what it was about, and Sabina said that it was the story of a nothing town in a nothing place in the 1800s, and the election of its member of the legislature, and a bit of extortion among candidates involving a mislaid love letter.

"You should read it. It's wickedly funny in places."

"I don't know if my Romanian is quite that good. Hard to catch the humor for a non-native speaker, especially if it's subtle."

"Your Romanian is fine. You should pick it up. I'm sure there are dozens of copies in every used bookstore. Like I said, every kid of a certain age had to read it."

We left the writers' busts and walked until the next bench. She sat without saying anything.

"Married?" she said to me.

"Getting right to the point, then."

"That wasn't an answer."

"No, not married."

"Ever married?"

"Once, yes," I said. I had to think for a second who I was when I was speaking to her, Alex Kovacs or Alex Kramer. Occupational hazard. In that I was Alex Kovacs, and in that she was at least tangentially involved with my anti-Communist cell, and in that I was becoming more and more interested in seeing what was beneath Sabina's blouse and figured a little sympathy wouldn't hurt, I told her a little about Manon and her death. And if I was going to burn in hell for using my dead wife, the only woman I had ever truly loved — used her for such purposes — well, it was a nice blouse. A lovely blouse, truly.

"Your turn," I said, after I was done.

"Not married."

"Not ever?"

"Once," she said. "The same as you, but different. Marius died during the war. Somewhere near Vilnius, but that's just a guess. Early 1943, also just a guess. That's when the telegram came. And he saved me even before he was drafted."

She stopped, stared off at the line of bushes across the path from our bench. In the silence, I heard some kids whooping behind us. We must have been closer to the paddle boats than I had thought.

"You see, I'm Jewish," Sabina said. "Marius was Catholic. Our families were against the wedding — my father didn't even come to the ceremony. He said, 'I'm not setting foot in that goddamned church.'"

"A priest married you?"

"Yeah. Funny, huh? The pastor was dead set against it, but one of his assistants, a young priest, just a kid. He could sense where all of this was headed — it was 1938, but as he said, 'You'd have to be blind not to see it.'"

She stopped again, stared.

"There was a young girl who had died about 10 years before," Sabina said. "A girl from the parish. Ana Barbu. Died of typhoid, age 14. Died, and the family moved away for a fresh start. And, well, the young priest supplied me with the works as far as Catholic documentation — baptismal certificate, first Holy Communion date, confirmation, the lot. He married us, and supplied the marriage certificate, too — all in the name of Ana Barbu.

"But Sabina?"

"If anyone ever asked, it was a family nickname," she said. "But no one ever did — the paperwork protected me just fine. Perfectly. And I found out later — from the young priest — that the pastor required, shall we say, a gratuity. That came from Marius. He never told me himself."

"And the roundups?"

"You know about them?"

"I've heard," I said. I couldn't explain how I had heard, how I had met a woman named Ana Radu while on a mission in Istanbul, a Romanian Jew, a terrorist fueled by revenge.

"They never touched me," Sabina said. "My mother was dead. My father..."

Her voice trailed off. And if I knew that I still lived it, it never ceased to amaze me how much the war still dominated peoples' lives in every country I visited. The shooting had stopped five years earlier, and the rebuilding had begun. There were parts of some cities I had seen — Vienna, Budapest, Tallinn — where you would never know about the war if you didn't already know. But that was the problem, because you did know. And if the facades were repaired and the walls painted over, well, there was no way to fix the cracks in the human beings who had survived. They really should have restarted the calendar, BH and AH. Before Hitler and After Hitler.

"I'm so lonely sometimes," she said. "You ever feel that?"

"Only always," I said.

More silence now. More silence than words. And if I knew where this was headed, and I knew it would be against Fritz's advice — no, his instructions — oh, well. Fritz's line was clear and consistent: whores only. And... oh, well.

"How's the local wine," I said, picking up the bottle and retrieving the corkscrew from my pocket.

"Better than the local food."

I looked at her, questioning.

"I know what you assholes say about our food," she said.

I thought about telling her Jake's line about "afterbirth on a plate," but decided against it. We sat on the park bench and drank the wine and then walked back to her apartment. Nothing had been decided verbally — we just walked, and then, about a second after the latch clicked, we started removing each other's clothing. Her blouse first. A lovely blouse, truly.

19

"There's more people this time," I said.

"Maybe because the weather's nicer," Bogdan said.

"If you say so."

"I have no idea why the fuck they come and do their gyrations. Just a theory." The final punctuation came in the form of a belch that, if I had lit a match, would have resulted in a conflagration that looked like the Hindenburg.

"Are you drunk?"

"A little," Bogdan said. "I think I'm entitled. You, too, for that matter."

The truth was, I had been drunk until noon. It was the night after we blew up an electrical transformer on the outskirts of the city — and if it left about 20 percent of Bucharest in darkness, well, like Bogdan said. It was a nice night.

We sat on the benches outside the chapel on Metropolitan Hill, waiting for the rest to show up for the debrief. Constantin was inside, kneeling and blessing himself.

"Where's your brother?"

"Young Florin has discovered pussy, it seems," Bogdan said.

"I was worried about the boy for a long time, until I found a torn-up old magazine under his mattress. In German. Some Nazi must have left it behind. It was one of those naturist magazines — lots of Gretas and Hildas playing volleyball with their Gretas and Hildas bouncing around in the sunshine. Unencumbered, shall we say. Good, clean fun."

"So..."

"Nothing wrong with him, just shy. I think this girl dragged him into the cloakroom at a café, and..."

"Good, clean fun," I said. For a few seconds, I was thinking about my times with Sabina — three times so far, not that I was counting.

Valentina, Jake and Peter arrived in order, and Florin arrived on a run just as Constantin emerged from the church service. Both Bogdan and I offered a dirty smile at Florin, and he angrily stared down his brother as he recognized that I had been let in on his female secret.

"I think he's about to sniff his fingers," I said, leaning in to Bogdan and whispering. He burst out laughing and, even though Florin had no idea what I had said, he began to blush.

I had been a part of the mission to blow up the electrical transformer. Suddenly, the rustiness of my skills was no longer an issue given the way Peter had botched things at Ploesti. It had always been bullshit — when they showed me the mechanics, even though the explosive was different, the fuses and the timers weren't any different from what I had worked with in France. Well, a little different — but two minutes of instruction made me more than familiar enough.

I couldn't tell if Peter resented my inclusion on the detail or if he welcomed it. I mean, for public consumption, he was appropriately offended.

"I don't need you to fucking hold my dick while I piss," he

said. It took every bit or restraint on my part not to say, "You mean, when you piss down your leg."

"Group effort — you can hold my dick, too," is what I said instead. Peter replied with a grunt. A few minutes later, the four of us arrived — no Florin this time, and no Jake again, and Valentina never seemed to come — Constantin and Bogdan tied up the single night watchman. It was a maneuver that required less skill than you might have thought, given that the watchman was asleep on a folding chair when we arrived, asleep and unarmed besides.

At which point, Peter and I were on stage. We had three minutes, according to the plan — although it was hard to understand the rush, given the single watchman. That was all we had seen on the reconnaissance, too, just the one guard — although a military vehicle of some sort did tend to drive by hourly, but on a varying schedule.

I thought three minutes was unnecessarily pushing it and told Constantin as much. He said, "A truck once an hour. Three minutes. That's a five percent chance of getting interrupted. That's plenty for me, thanks."

"But five or six minutes would give us..."

"Christ, are you explosives people all so temperamental."

So, three minutes it was. Honestly, it was plenty for two men to arm two bombs apiece. The problem was, Peter froze when the time came. What happened was, he handed me the materials out of the knapsack and I put them together and set the timers. The system was efficient enough — although Peter's hands were shaking uncontrollably for much of the time — but it wasn't as planned. It was a rush to get the four bombs assembled and the timers set in three minutes.

"Three minutes, 10 seconds," Constantin said when the two of us arrived at the place where he and Bogdan were hiding — behind a small concrete pillbox that contained who-knew-what.

"For fuck's sake," I said.

"Ten seconds is ten seconds," Constantin said. He wasn't smiling.

The bombs, if I had coordinated the timers properly, would blow at five minutes after I began. As it turned out, three of them went at almost exactly the same time, and the fourth about 10 seconds later.

"Four-for-fucking-four," Bogdan said. He ignored Peter, who was right next to him, and reached across to clap me on the back.

"Good team," I said.

Peter and Constantin said nothing. And the way Constantin told the others as we sat on the benches on Metropolitan Hill, it had all been about planning and teamwork. And if I enjoyed the feeling, the feeling I remembered from the Resistance days, the glow of a successful mission, I also remembered why I had drunk so much the previous night. It wasn't in celebration — well, only partially. It was also in disappointment — because now, through two missions, I had seen nothing and learned nothing that would explain the failure of the mission that had seen me come to Bucharest in the first place. This second one, I had been in on every element of it from reconnaissance to ka-boom, and I had seen nothing but solid planning and decision-making.

Fritz had sent me, most of all, to find out what the Americans were up to. And, well, all I knew was that Jake was a blowhard and Peter was an incompetent. Neither of those things was particularly nefarious, though. Blowhard was embedded in the genetics of Americans, after all, and incompetence probably afflicted about 50 percent of human beings. And whatever else, there was nothing about the people in the cell that suggested anything other than what they were — a group of anti-Communist true believers who were trying, at a minimum, to be a pain in the government's ass.

I was nowhere and I knew it. Still, the afterglow of the mission did soften that disappointment. And as we stood up to leave after Constantin's debriefing, I looked over at Florin and then poked Bogdan in the ribs and said, "Look."

At which point, we both watched as his little brother was, indeed, sniffing his fingers.

20

"Alex, walk with me," Constantin said. The others scattered, and I played follow the leader.

"Let's get a glass of tea," he said. "My cousin has a shop. It's not far."

We began walking away from the only path I had ever used to reach the top of Metropolitan Hill. I always considered that path, the one that led back toward the center of the city, as the main entrance to the complex of buildings on the plateau. We were headed a different way, farther back and over to the right.

Constantin was next to me, and I guess I wasn't paying attention, because I continued walking straight for a couple of strides before I noticed he had turned off.

"Here," he said.

"Here what?"

"You've never seen this?" he said, and then I got to his side and realized what he was talking about. It was a small staircase, narrow and kind of hidden but, well, not really hidden. It was there in plain sight if you were looking for it — but you had to be looking for it, if that made any sense.

I looked down. It was tight and it had a couple of turns in it

— more bends than turns, to be honest. There appeared to be some fences and gates on either side that separated the steps from some yard space. Nearer to the bottom, the openness of the chain-link fences and the grassy yards was replaced by the sides of houses on each side. The whole thing might have been four feet wide, four feet maybe, with a lot of uneven concrete steps separated by a few landings along the way.

"It would be tougher in a half-hour, when it's really dark out," Constantin said, leading the way. We were single file by necessity. It wasn't that far, maybe a hundred steps or so. We were down into the little street, among a cluster of houses, in less than two minutes.

"Just down here," he said, pointing to where the little street dumped into one that was a little busier. The tea shop had a sign over the door that said, "Ciobanu."

"Shepherd," Constantin said.

"Huh."

"Ciobanu means shepherd," he said. For some reason, he was suddenly speaking German. But it was only for that single translation. We were back to Romanian after that.

Constantin entered the tea shop and there were hugs all around, hugs and rapid talking and joshing that left me underwater. After we sat down and the tea was delivered, though, we were on our own and Constantin was speaking just slowly enough for me to keep up.

"You're very good," he said.

"I practiced with phonograph records and a teacher."

"I mean with the bombs. Your Romanian is borderline shit by comparison to the bombs."

He cracked himself up and laughed long and loud. Then, he said, "No, your Romanian isn't shit. Very good, in fact."

We drank the tea out of glasses with silver spoons inside that grabbed enough of the heat to keep the glass from cracking. Had to be real silver, though. I sometimes wondered where little shops like this got the money.

"So, what do you think of our little operation?" Constantin said. Right to it, then.

"Things are very well-planned."

"Said the ass-kisser."

"No, seriously."

"No, seriously, you've been around the block. So, what do you think?" he said.

I had not anticipated any of this — not the tea shop, not the private conversation, not this particular line of questioning. And the truth was, I really didn't know what to think — there hadn't been enough time, and I just hadn't learned enough about the operation or the people. I did have my initial impressions — Constantin seemed like a caring leader, Valentina a bitch, Jake a blowhard, Peter an incompetent, Bogdan a fine drinking companion, Florin an earnest little brother in need of nurturing. But they were just that, impressions that lacked depth or color or nuance.

"I wasn't kidding about the planning," I said. In that, I was telling the truth. I could find no fault in how the operations at Ploesti or the electrical transformer had been mapped out.

"My two operations," I said.

"But what about the other one? You liked the planning on that one?"

Constantin was referring to the one that got Andrei, my Gehlen predecessor, killed up near the Hungary border.

I didn't answer for several seconds. Then — again, stick with the truth — I said, "It's just, why was he by himself?"

Constantin sipped his tea and then kind of half grimaced and half smiled at the same time.

"He wasn't supposed to be," he said.

I stared back and tried to betray nothing.

"The plan was different," he said. "He was to have had help. But at the last minute — poof, he was gone, gone by himself. He hadn't liked the plan from the start, and when he saw an opportunity to ditch his partner — Valentina — well, poof."

"What hadn't he liked?" I said.

"That it was Valentina going with him. We had worked it out among the three of us — this was a smaller group than the usual. No need to involve the others. And, well, the chauvinistic idiot. She might be better with a pistol than any of us. But, no. Your former colleague, well, he thought he was bulletproof. Let's just say he sometimes used to think with his balls more than his brains. You know the type?"

I nodded. I did know the type because, well, because I could be the type at times — not the chauvinist part but the I-know-best part. It was at least some of the reason I liked to work by myself, some of the reason I was so uncomfortable on this assignment.

We finished our tea, and one of Constantin's cousins arrived without being summoned and offered fresh glasses. We drank them, and Constantin went through the whole electrical transformer mission again, step by step. When he got to the setting of the explosives, he said, "Was he any help?" I knew he was referring to Peter.

"We were a good team," I said.

"You take the piss and he holds your dick — I'm pretty much correct about that, right? Or maybe he just unbuttons your fly?"

"I don't know—"

"Stop protecting him. This is too important for that. You were leading and he was following. I saw how you took control of the whole thing. I saw what he was doing, which was pretty much nothing."

"Not nothing."

"All he was doing was, well, he was just handing you the shit from the bag. You know it and I know it."

"You don't miss much."

"Can't afford to, not in my position," Constantin said, and then he thought for a second and commenced with a long speech about the evils of Communism and the importance of civil resistance during these times.

He said, "Every life has a time, and this is mine. I really believe that there's a small window in every person's life where they have an opportunity to make a significant difference. Well, this is my time, and this is my place, and this group we have put together is my chance to do something memorable, something meaningful. And I can't blow it — I won't blow it — just to save some hard feelings over some incompetent American."

"Even if it's the Americans who are supplying the money and—"

"—and you now that how?"

"I work for people who, well, let's just say they understand where the money comes from in this little battle in which we are all engaged, not just here but..."

I had said enough. Constantin nodded. We finished up and left the tea house after an extensive set of departure hugs and rib-jabbing and fast-talking that I couldn't manage to absorb. At the bottom of the street, he clapped me on the back and pointed me back in the direction of my rooming house near the university. Back there, I radioed an account of the meeting to Fritz, or whoever was listening to the radio on Fritz's behalf.

This had been the first explanation I had received of the botched operation near the Hungary border. It sounded plausible enough. It was what we had guessed back in Vienna before it all started — that sending Andrei alone had made no sense, and that he likely had gone full-cowboy and paid the price. And if that was the case, well, wasn't my work in Bucharest done — or, at least, nearly done?

I had no idea what the reaction would be on the other end. After I sent the message, though, I sat there and waited with some hopeful anticipation. This might be it. This message might be my ticket home.

Ten minutes, nothing.

Fifteen minutes, nothing.

Eighteen minutes, finally. But the reply was just one word. One hope-crushing word: "Received."

21

A note had been slipped under my door at the Athenee Palace — by Benny himself. "It seemed important," he told me, with a bit of a conspiratorial whisper.

The note was from Sofia Popescu. She was back in the city but only for the day. She proposed a meeting near the train station at 3 p.m. Her train back to Resita was at 4, and if I couldn't make it, she would try again in a week or so.

I was waiting on a bench in a little, nondescript park behind the station when Sofia arrived. I stood, and she greeted me with a hug that lasted a half-second longer than I might have anticipated. Whatever.

The look in her eyes was so hopeful. They asked the question for her.

"Not good news, not bad news," I said.

"What does that mean?"

"The man I've been working with, he brought back a list. Your husband's name wasn't on it."

I hadn't noticed that Sofia had pulled a handkerchief out of her pocket, not until she buried her face in it. After maybe 10 seconds of long, low sobs, she looked at me. The tears had smeared her makeup, and snot dripped from her left nostril. I pointed at it, and she wiped her nose. Then she sobbed again.

"So, what's the good news?"

"I didn't say there was good news. But, well, this is not the end of the story. That's why it wasn't good news and it wasn't bad news. This was just a first pass of his sources. He found some of the names I was looking for but not nearly all of them. He believes strongly that he can find some more."

And if I had made up the part about "believes strongly?" It seemed the least I could do. I was still looking into her eyes when I said it, and the effect was visible, palpable — along with the fact that she took my hand in hers when I said it.

"I've also, well, I've been able to add a financial incentive," I said. "There will be additional money included in the transaction if he can find your husband in one of the camps."

"Additional money?"

I nodded. She reached down for her purse began to root around for what I presumed was the same wad of money she had brought to our first meeting.

"No," I said, and this time I grabbed her hand.

"Are you sure?"

"Yes, I'm sure."

"Additional money. You did that for me?"

I looked down.

At which point, Sofia Popescu, who had been sobbing over the fate of her lost husband just 30 seconds earlier, moved closer to me on the bench, took my face in her two hands, then hugged me for a good bit, and then allowed her right hand to fall from the back of my shoulder. It fell into my lap, where it remained for the duration of the hug.

A hug that ended with her whispering into my ear, "I have an hour before my train."

First Sabina, now Sofia. Two lonely women interested in sex

for sex's sake. I was not new to the concept, not through personal experience and also by general knowledge. Christ, Leon had written the book on the care and feeding of lonely, horny women. I had told him, more than once, that if he wrote a book about that, it would sell a lot more than the history of the French Resistance that he believed would be his greatest achievement if he ever finished it. And he said, "The problem is, well, it's too simple. You listen to them, pay attention to them, and they can't fuck you fast enough. I could come up with a good title: *Undress Them with Your Ears*. But after that, well, there's nothing left to say."

I managed to extricate myself from the hug and made up some bullshit about an appointment back at the Athenee Palace. Sofia replied with a half-pout, and then a smile, and then another hug with hands in the appropriate places. She walked toward the train station and I walked toward the hotel. I liked to think that she thought about me and smiled on the ride home. I know I thought about her and smiled, especially when I got into the shower. I had a quiet night that night, just the one drink in the English Bar. It was only when I was getting into bed when I realized just how disappointed in me Leon would be if I told him the truth about walking away, and how proud he would be if I embroidered a tale about rushing across the street to one of the hot-sheets railroad hotels across from the station. So, I was embroidering as I fell asleep.

22

The Dancing Waters was dead when I walked in. Sabina was behind the counter, perched on the same stool, reading the same book. She looked up and smiled at me when the door slammed, and I smiled back. But I was late, and I pointed at my wristwatch and then gestured toward the back room. The smile this time was accompanied by a raised middle finger.

When I walked in, the group was in mid-argument. This one was interesting. It wasn't Jake being a know-it-all-American, and it wasn't Bogdan being a smart ass. Those were undercard fights compared to what I walked in on — the main event, the two heavyweight of the group, Constantin vs. Valentina.

When I sat down at the table, she barely looked up to acknowledge my late arrival with a snarl.

"Sorry," I said.

"Fuck your sorries," she said. "And fuck this whole thing. You want this asshole to be a part of it, and it's... it's... it's less than a pimple on anybody's ass. It's absurd. It's a ridiculous risk."

"It's not ridiculous," Constantin said.

"Not a pimple."

"You're wrong."

Then Constantin looked at me and laid out the proposed mission. My new best tea-drinking friend was obviously trying to recruit an ally. I had no idea how the rest felt — they seemed to be enjoying the show, especially Bogdan — but the attention he was paying to me suggested that Dear Leader needed another voice on his side.

"You know the Telephone Palace, right?" Constantin said.

I shrugged.

"For fuck's sake," Valentina said.

Constantin said the Telephone Palace was a big building on Victoriei, and that it — not surprisingly — housed the telephone exchanges for the entire city, as well as some business offices.

"It's a distinctive building — I'm sure you've seen it," he said.

For the second time, I shrugged.

"Why are you even bothering?" Valentina said. Constantin mumbled a quick, "Please fucking shut up for 30 seconds," and then gave her a quick stare, and then he turned his attention back to me.

And I said, "We're going to blow up a big, tall building? There isn't enough dynamite in the country to do that. Just, like, so you know."

"We're not going to blow up the building," Constantin said.

"No, we're just going to pop the pimple on its ass," Valentina said.

This time, Constantin shut her up with the longest, coldest stare I had seen him deliver. Valentina had always been the silent partner in the leadership group, the one who hectored everyone about the details, the bitch. I had never sensed any divide between them — and, hell, everybody else thought they were sleeping together, so I don't imagine they had sensed a schism, either. But here it was, and maybe they were right about the two of them being a couple. That stare seemed like the kind only a couple could exchange — full of personal knowledge and shared experiences. And, anyway, Valentina did shut up.

"We're not blowing up the building — not all of it, anyway," Constantin said. "We just want to knock out some of the exchanges, as many as we can hit in five minutes. Tiny explosions, just enough to fuck with the control panels. Three, four, five of them. If we're lucky, we'll knock out half the city — but it will be five minutes and out. Not 10 minutes. Not six. Five minutes and out."

I said nothing. No one did. Finally, it was Bogdan who tiptoed into the void and said, "Boss, it does seem like..."

"Like what, funny man?"

Bogdan was surprised at the retort, and maybe a little intimidated, but he plowed ahead.

"Like a big risk for a small reward," Bogdan said.

Constantin then went around the room. He looked at Florin, and the kid's eyes dropped. He looked at Peter, and when he started to say, "It might be hard," Constantin cut him off.

"Hard to carry the knapsack and hand the devices to Alex? Jesus Christ — a child could do it, and the child would have less of a chance of pissing himself."

Peter's eyes, like Florin's, fell. That left Jake.

"Fuck it, why not?" he said.

"A goddamned ringing endorsement," Valentina said.

It had only been a few minutes, but the confrontation seemed to have sapped everyone. Valentina passed around the bottle of rocket fuel — and it was interesting that she handed it to Constantin first after pouring her own. Even in the middle of a vicious argument, there were still protocols, it seemed.

After everyone had poured, Constantin looked at me and said, "Well?"

I had been hoping to slide through without giving an opinion, but no such luck. I attempted a straddle.

"Look, I don't think it's just a bullshit stunt like some of you do," I said. "But there will be a risk, clearly, seeing as how it's right in the middle of the city. I guess, for me, it will all come down to the soundness of the plan. The last two plans I've been a part of, well, they've been excellent — well-thought-out, all of the contingencies and risks laid out in a realistic manner. I've been really comfortable with both of those. In my life of doing this work, I've been involved in some wild-ass capers, missions that were long shots from the jump. But Ploesti and the electrical transformer — not wild-ass, not at all. Like I said, very sound. Very realistic. The opportunities were clearly laid out, as were the potential pitfalls. But, unless I missed something because I was late, there isn't really a plan for this one yet, just an idea about the Telephone Tower. So with this one, well, I don't know enough yet to have an opinion — not a valid opinion, anyway."

I took a quick peek at Constantin out of the side of my eye. A quick peek, and what registered was just a hint of a smile on the leader's face. I had given him what he needed, and just that quickest of glances told me that he was grateful.

"That's all fair," Constantin said. "And look — I hear what all of you have said. We've been yelling about it, and maybe I've sounded like a know-it-all asshole..."

"Maybe?" Bogdan said. He was smiling, and Constantin smiled back.

"Whatever I sounded like, I do respect your opinions. I am hearing them. But Alex is right — it's not a bullshit stunt. Every time we hit them, big or small, it's a benefit. Every time, whatever we do, is like a drip-drip-drip on their consciousness. It makes them question everything. It saps their confidence. It frays their nerves. It's worth it, every bit of it."

Constantin stopped talking and drained his glass in one.

"But, look, Alex is also right about this: it all depends on the quality of the plan."

At which point, he ordered the first pass of a reconnaissance mission at the Telephone Tower for three nights later. The bottle of rocket fuel was passed again, emptying it, and everyone drank quickly. Jake and Peter, the two Americans, left first. Then, Bogdan and Florin — and as Bogdan walked by, Constantin stood up and hugged him. I still had a sip left, and I was going to stop to see Sabina besides, so I waited them out — and, yes, Constantin and Valentina did leave together, even it was a wordless departure. Through the silence, though, our gazes met — and Constantin did offer what I clearly felt was a 'thank you' with his eyes.

23

Sabina wouldn't be able to close the café for two more hours, and she said she felt lousy besides. Some kind of bug. So I walked back to the rooming house alone and couldn't shake the notion that I was wasting my time. With each day, my homesickness had grown. And now, this Telephone Palace business — despite what I had said to the group, well, if it wasn't a bullshit stunt or a pimple on the government's ass, it had grown up in the same neighborhood.

I had lived that life in France. I had been a part of Resistance groups that blew up fuel depots that were resupplied within hours, or dynamited train trestles that were rebuilt in days. We were like Constantin, convinced that the drip-drip-drip of our sabotage efforts would have an effect on the Nazis who occupied France — and maybe they did a little. But the truth was that the Nazis might have hated occupying Paris in the end, and we might have worn them down to a certain degree, but they didn't leave until the Americans showed up. One of the unspoken reasons why the Nazi soldiers looked so worn out in Paris at the end was because the demands of the Russian front had led to all of the bright, young, smiling-on-a-poster German soldiers who arrived in Paris in 1940 being shipped east, their places filled by aging second-line soldiers. But even with that, they would have dealt with our bullshit sabotage indefinitely without the Americans.

Leon and I got drunk one night in Montmartre after the liberation, vomit-in-the-gutter drunk during those first hours where you had to shoulder your way between people to find a space along the curb to throw up — that's how drunk everybody was. And in the middle of all of that celebratory whirlwind that lasted for days — get drunk, throw up, find a girl, have sex, grab a shower, repeat — Leon said, "I'm a journalist. I'm not a romantic about any of this shit. And I'm proud of what I did, what we did together, and I'd do all of it again. There's stuff that happened — and you know it, too — that we'll be desperate to forget. That's the only thing I've prayed for in years, decades — that I'll be able to forget. But, well, like I said. I'm not a romantic. I'm a realist. And I can be proud, yes. And I can see our work with the Resistance, well, there was an honesty to it. Honesty and nobility. That's the word — nobility. And I will believe that until I die. But the truth is, we didn't do shit. We'd still be blowing up railroad crossings, and the Nazis would still be repairing them the next day, if G.I. Fucking Joe hadn't showed up in Normandy."

"And the Russians from the other way," I said.

"Yeah," Leon said. "Fuck them, but yeah."

I thought of that conversation as I walked back to the rooming house. One more transformer, one more telephone exchange — for what? What were we really accomplishing? Anything?

This game was being played so far over our heads, it wasn't funny. The Americans were all hot to fight the Communists at every step, to continue to develop and nurture grass roots opposition — and the Gehlen Org was the Americans' useful tool and sometimes their only tool — but for what? Seriously, for what? I had done this in Istanbul, and Budapest, and Estonia, and now in Bucharest — and my successes could be measured only with the aid of a microscope. What was the point here, other than to leave behind a trail of bodies — some who deserved it but many of whom were innocents? What was the goddamned point?

The Communists were in firm control in Romania, and the Soviets had supplied them with their game plan and their advisors, and we were fucking gnats against them. We were like midges in the summer. And, yes, midges can spoil a walk in the country in July. They can make you spend an afternoon continually swatting them from the air in front of your face and then an evening measuring the futility of it all by examining your handkerchief after you blow your nose. But it's only an annoyance. It's temporary and avoidable enough. And that's what Constantin and his little group were — midges. Gnats. A bother and nothing more than a bother. We could ruin a picnic, but bring down a government? The whole thing was laughable when you thought about it that way.

I'd had enough to drink that I decided to try to be a bit more explicit about my desire to get the fuck out of Bucharest in a radio transmission to Fritz. I'd already sent what Constantin had said about how Andrei the cowboy went off on his own in the mission near the border that got him killed, off on his own because he wouldn't work with Valentina. It seemed believable enough. Meanwhile, the two missions I had participated in — at least the reconnaissance — were well-planned and uneventful. I had no idea what I was hoping to discover anymore, no idea why I was still in Bucharest.

I sent all of that in a message that was as tight as I could make it while still conveying my desire to leave. And it was a legitimate use of the radio because I also sent details about the Telephone Tower mission.

The last two words of the message were, "Request parachute." That was my shorthand for, "Get me the fuck out of here." It wasn't a pre-planned thing, that particular message, but I assumed that the meaning was obvious enough.

The response came within two minutes:

"Remain in place."

To send a second message, where I just whined some more, went against the established protocols for radio transmissions. The thing wasn't a toy, and there were risks — again, I had no idea how much the technology of radio detection had improved since the years of those goofy Nazi vans with the rotating antennas on the roof. Still, I did it anyway.

The message was only three short sentences:

"Anti-Communist cell appears as advertised. Risk-reward of continuing seems out of whack. Request parachute."

The reply came 10 minutes later:

"Remain in place and remember the task... to find out what the Americans are up to."

I thought about sending a third message but realized that I was already one beyond what I was permitted. Fritz was more explicit in that second reply than I had expected, and it did refocus me a little. The Americans. Find out more about the Americans, about Jake and Peter, about the blowhard and the incompetent, the Yankee odd couple. Find out if our paymasters had some kind of agenda that wasn't obvious.

"Fuck it," is what I muttered to myself as I hid the radio again between the mattress and the box spring. Fritz wasn't going to be pushing my ejector button or sending a parachute anytime soon. That much was plain.

24

Sabina was feeling better the next day and suggested an afternoon walk before her shift at the café. She said she wanted to show me something.

"Some history," she said.

My reply was apparently less than enthusiastic, and she said, "What? You hate history, too?"

"What do you mean, too?"

"The literary busts in the park, you could not have cared less. Now, I offer history and you sneer."

"I didn't sneer."

"Close enough. Are you a complete anti-intellectual?"

What I wanted to say, in the moment, was that I thought my job in this relationship, if you wanted to call it a relationship, was to be an available penis — and that hers was the inverse. Or converse, or reverse, or obverse — I never could keep any of them straight. Maybe I was an anti-intellectual.

"Is that how you see me?" I said. "As someone who drinks too much, and belches, and scratches himself?"

"Well..."

"Drinking too much, and belching, and scratching all have a

place in my life, but so does history," I said. Then I belched on command as a form of punctuation. That got Sabina to smile, and then we were off.

It wasn't too far of a walk. We were a block away and she said, "Look." I did look, and what I saw was a bunch of the new Commie-style buildings that were either newly built or under construction.

"What? Ugly boxes?" I said.

"Yes, ugly boxes. But more than that. Come."

We walked closer, and then I saw where we were headed — to an old synagogue, what Sabina called "the Great Synagogue."

"The ugly boxes—"

"They're camouflage," she said. "They hide the synagogue, isolate it. You can see it if you're looking, but it's as if you're trying to look through the trees to find a hut in a forest clearing. There, but not there."

The door was unlocked and we went inside. An old man was sitting in a chair just inside the door, half asleep. But the flash of sunlight and the squeak of the hinges woke him, and he handed me a yarmulke from the stack on a little table.

It was dark and gold and elaborate and haunting. We were the only people inside. Sabina led me around the perimeter, not saying anything about what we were looking at. She only talked about the past.

"So, I know you know about the pogrom."

I nodded.

"June 27 and June 28, 1941," she said. "Just, well, it never affected me because I was Ana Barbu with the baptismal certificate and the confirmation date and the marriage certificate to prove it. But..."

She stopped. Her voice caught.

"You know the thing I'll never forget?" she said. "It was the posters that they slapped on the walls. It seemed like they were suddenly everywhere, and they stayed up for years, it felt like. I bet you could still find one if you looked hard enough. There was this one poster especially. It said, 'Romanians! Each kike killed is a dead Communist. The time for revenge is now!' Exclamation point after 'Romanian.' Exclamation point after 'now.' God, it's what I always see first when I close my eyes and think about it, the exclamation points."

There were a couple of folding chairs set up in one corner of the sanctuary. I had no idea if they still did services, or what. Anyway, we sat down.

"But that's not why I brought you here," Sabina said. "Not to tell you about the pogrom, or about the five-year-old girl who was one of the group that was skinned alive in a kosher slaughterhouse and hung from meat hooks. No, not that. I brought you here to tell you about something different, something better, something even darker, maybe. I wanted to tell you about revenge."

Sabina reached over and grabbed my hand. She squeezed, and I squeezed in return. She smiled, and I think I did, too.

"Revenge," she said. "It was later, after the Nazis were gone. It was in April of 1945, Passover. It was right here in this sanctuary, in a circle of rickety folding chairs."

By then, by my estimation, Sabina would have been in her late twenties. Her husband had been dead for two years, give or take.

"A friend brought me," she said. "There was a group of a dozen people here, all maybe a little younger than me or about the same age. They had come from all over, survivors of the Nazis. Some hid in the sewers of Vilnius, others, well..."

"All Jews, then?"

"All Jews, even me," she said.

The smile was weaker this time. I squeezed her hand but there was no squeeze in reply.

"They called themselves the *nokmim*. It's Hebrew for "avengers." And these dozen people — mostly men, but a few women — had decided that their task, their calling, was to get revenge for the six million Jews whom the Nazis had slaughtered. They thought it was only fair, only just, that they kill six million Germans in return."

She looked at me and stopped. I guessed that my mouth was open at that point.

"I've shocked you," Sabina said.

"Certainly surprised me."

"They were serious. The way the figured they could do it most efficiently was to poison the water supply in the big cities. They mentioned Munich, Berlin and some others. Nuremberg, I think, because that's where the Nazis had their big meetings."

Part of me wanted to tell her that I knew about the meetings. Mostly, I knew that, from my days as a traveling sales rep for my family's mine, not to schedule client visits near Nuremberg at the time of the annual Nazifest because it was impossible to get a hotel room.

But, well, I just listened and tried to keep my mouth from falling wide open again.

"They were so alive," she said. "So motivated. So right in their beliefs. I was electrified. Those few days, I'll never forget them."

"But, well..."

"They left here after a couple of weeks. I think they were headed to Italy — something to do with being able to trade counterfeit Allied money there for cash. I forget. But they were gone."

"But, like, it never happened, right? I mean, we would have heard, and I haven't heard."

"Nothing," Sabina said. "Nothing yet."

"You still think?"

"Nothing yet," she said, and this time, the smile was big and joyful.

We sat there for a few more minutes. It was such a wild story. The next time I talked to Fritz, face-to-face, I had to remember to ask him what he might know.

After a bit, I asked Sabina the only question I could think of. Well, I started to ask.

"Did you ever—"

"Consider going with them?" she said.

I nodded.

"In my head, maybe."

"But?"

"But only in my head," she said.

25

The guy working security at the building behind the Telephone Palace knew we were coming and let us in with a nod. Whether he had been paid off, or was a true believer, or both, didn't matter much to me. It had been arranged, and the guy let us in and then escorted us to a fifth-floor office of some insurance company.

"Pisser's down the hall," he said. "Don't bother flushing — nobody's here but, well, no sense making any extra noise. Leave from the same door when you're done, even if I'm not there. In fact, I probably won't be here — I have to make the rounds every hour. Cleaning crew gets here at 5. Anything happens, you've never met me — you've never seen me — and I don't know shit. Here..."

With that, the guard reached into his pocket and handed me a small fabric bag. Inside were several thick bits of wire of varying lengths — but thicker than wire and thinner than, say, a nail.

"Lock picks," the guard said. "In case you're caught, that's how you got in. On the way out, toss them under the chair where I sit. Got it?"

With that, we rolled a couple of chairs closer to the window and looked down on the back of the Telephone Tower. Jake, Bogdan and me.

"What exactly did Constantin say?" I asked.

Bogdan and Jake both spoke at once, and then they both stopped, and then they both started again at the same time, and then Bogdan said, "After you, asshole."

"He said there's only one guard at 2 a.m.," Jake said.

"One guard on the outside, one on the inside," Bogdan said.

"Like I was going to say," Jake said.

"And how does he know that?" I said.

The two of them looked at each other.

"He just fucking knows, I guess," Jake said.

It was about 12:30 p.m., and there were two guards at the back door — bored soldiers leaning on wooden crates and smoking cigarettes, their rifles propped next to them against the crates. We couldn't hear them — the windows in the insurance office were closed — but you could see them laughing and gesticulating. Smoking, telling jokes, killing time. Soldiers doing the soldier thing — that is, killing time during what otherwise would be a mind-numbing tour.

"Why Palace?" I said. "I mean, it's a nice enough building and all, but palace? Is there a King of Telephones in Romania that nobody ever told me about in history class?"

"It's a palace because it was built by Americans, for Americans," Jake said. "Made in the fucking U-S-of-A."

"It was built in Romania, by Romanians," Bogdan said.

"It was built from American plans for the American company that operates the telephones in this godforsaken backwater."

Bogdan clenched his fists but went quiet. I said, "What are you talking about?"

"They couldn't run their own telephone system, so they sold

it to International Telephone and Telegraph. I-T-T equals U-S-A. Their executives run the thing from here. The building was built for them. Art Deco style, they tell me. Look at it in the daylight sometimes. It's probably nothing special by New York standards, but it wouldn't look out of place on the corner of Fifth Avenue and 50th Street. It's the sweetest, most modern building in this whole shithole country — the tallest building in the city, which means the tallest building in the country. A palace. An American palace."

"Shut him up, Alex, or I will," Bogdan said.

Jake declared victory with a grin and, indeed, shut up. We went back to the task at hand. Every few minutes, somebody came out of the back door. Sometimes it was a worker wearing overalls bearing the acronym S.A.R.T, which was what the Romanian telephone company was called. Usually, though, it was another soldier who was undoubtedly going off shift. Every time the door opened, we were able to catch a glimpse of the inside guard, sitting behind a desk with a logbook in front of him. That guard's rifle was propped against the wall behind where he was sitting.

"All pretty casual," Bogdan said.

"Yeah, seems like bullshit duty to me," I said.

"It's bullshit because there's nothing worth guarding," Bogdan said.

"Are we really going to fucking do this again?" Jake said. "The argument's been had. You lost. Fucking get over it."

At 1 a.m., one of the outside soldiers went inside. Again, in the second or two the door was open, we could see him reach into what appeared to be a rack of time cards that was hanging on the wall. He was going to punch out. I had never heard of soldiers punching out but, well, whatever. Thirty second later, he and a half-dozen other soldiers all came out, their tours undoubtedly over. One of them looked over his shoulder as he walked away and shouted something to the single remaining soldier, who responded with a raised middle finger.

"Now what?" Bogdan said,

"We wait," Jake said.

"For what?"

"For 2 o'clock."

"No, 3 o'clock," I said.

"The mission is at 2," Jake said. "Constantin said 2. I was listening. He said 2."

"And we're waiting until 3, just to be sure," I said. "I might not know a lot about you guys or about Bucharest, but this is my business. I guarantee that I've done more of these things than the rest of the group combined."

"Yeah, in France," Jake said.

"Bullets rip through your skin the same in Limoges or Bucharest. Explosives go ka-boom the same way, whatever language is written on the box. And I say we wait. Shit can happen, delays can happen. We wait until 3."

"Fuck me," Bogdan said.

Those were the last words any of us said for an hour. We took turns at the window every 10 minutes or so, working out a wordless surveillance rotation — me, Jake, Bogdan; me, Jake, Bogdan. After his second stint at the window, Bogdan left the office, presumably to use the bathroom — a presumption confirmed by the sound of a flushing toilet. It startled Jake and me.

When Bogdan returned, Jake said, "The guy said not to flush."

"Trust me," Bogdan said.

I started laughing. Jake went to the door to listen for footsteps and was back in a few seconds.

"Nothing," he said.

"Trust me," Bogdan said. "If I had left that behind, there would have been a federal investigation."

"Fucking animal," Jake said. "It's the goddamned food."

"Or if not a federal investigation, well, it was a magnificent bit of work. True craftsmanship. Perhaps a presidential commendation instead."

"To go with your farting contest ribbon from school," I said.

"We would have to clear a whole shelf for them in my parents' house," Bogdan said.

At 2 o'clock, we all gathered around the window and watched the guard at the back door of the Telephone Palace. He sat, and he smoked, and he stood up, and he stretched his legs, and he smoked, and he half ducked behind the wooden crates to take a leak, and he smoked. He opened the back door at about 2:15 and left it propped open for a few minutes while he chatted with the inside guard. For what it was worth, the inside guy had his feet on the desk and his chair leaned back the whole time. He might have been asleep when the door opened.

By 2:20, the single soldier was back outside, sitting on the wooden crates, smoking. The rifle went untouched throughout, and it remained untouched when we left the insurance office at 3:05. And it was all the same, with only insignificant variations, when we repeated the surveillance two nights later.

26

I tried to get back to the Athenee Palace every day if I could — if for no other reason than to mess up the bed and make it appear as if it had been slept in. I tried to get back to the rooming house every day, too, in the hope that Ion would hear me on the steps. But if there was a reason that visiting both was impossible, I tried to get back to the Athenee Palace as my first choice. The main reason was that I knew the hotel chambermaids would be reporting about the state of my room to the Securitate — like, with 90 percent certainty — but I was still hopeful that Ion was just a funny old man and nothing more than that. I might have been kidding myself, but whatever. I was just playing the percentages — 90-10 versus, say, 50-50.

The other reason I preferred the hotel was the English Bar. It was the closest thing to my old life that I had experienced in a while. Back when, back in the days when I traveled around Germany and Austria servicing the clients of the Kovacs Mining Company, I had an English Bar in every city where I traveled, a place to unwind with a proper cocktail. I had a favorite place for a Manhattan in every stop along my route — just as I had a favorite hotel, and a favorite train, and a favorite dark club populated by enterprising women. They were for the clients, the enterprising women. Well, primarily for the clients.

It was a mindlessly splendid life I led, back before the war, back when all I cared about was adding 10 percent to the client's order, and booking passage on the *Orient Express* to and from Cologne, and fiddling my expenses as my Uncle Otto had taught me, and about the enterprising women. And if I felt a little empty inside, and if I could never seem to manage a real relationship with a real woman, well, there was always the *Orient Express*.

And, well, after Radu made me a Manhattan without asking, after I took the first sip, I could close my eyes for a second and pretend I was in Dresden in 1935 at the Excelsior after an afternoon-long sales call at Kreitzler Steel. There, at the Excelsior, I would be fortifying myself with two Manhattans before the night ahead — kind of an easy night, actually, in that old Jürgen Kreitzler had simple needs: one girl, blonde, age 20-30, average weight, fin. All a part of the Kovacs Mining Company service.

I actually laughed out loud when I realized that I still remembered old Jürgen Kreitzler's preferences in Dresden, and that, even 15 years later, I could recall the same along my former circuit of clients from Mainz (two girls, one fat), to Stuttgart (one girl, one man, easily accomplished with the proper compensation), to Saarbrücken (one black woman, which required an advance telephone call and a week's notice).

"What's so funny?" Radu said, interrupting my journey into the past.

"Oh, nothing."

He shrugged and walked away to tend to a man sitting at the other end of the bar. It was when I was half turned, watching him walk away, when the man in the black suit took the stool to my right.

"Herr Kramer," he said.

It took me a half-second to remember who I was — Alex Kramer, not Alex Kovacs. The momentary confusion must have shown on my face.

"Herr Alex Kramer, yes?"

"Yes, yes," I said. "I guess I was just startled that you spoke to me in German. Have we met?"

"We have not," the black suit said, switching to Romanian. He introduced himself as Mihai Stoica — Captain Mihai Stoica of the Securitate.

"May I call you Alex?" he said. Then, without waiting for an answer, he continued, "You have been a hotel guest for several weeks now, Alex, have you not?"

I nodded. Radu came over and asked Stoica if he wanted a drink. Stoica replied with a quick shake of his head and a glare that Radu understood instantly. He left us and returned to the customer at the other end of the bar.

When I was nervous, I tended to revert to my old salesman routine. Back then, knowing how to babble about anything for a period of time was probably the top skill required for the job. I could give you the short, medium or long dissertation on magnesite, our mining product. Or the weather. Or the *Orient Express*. Or whatever.

It was harder in this life, picking a suitable topic, but the skill — it was like muscle memory. And I had started with a monologue about Manhattans — rye versus bourbon, as a starter — when Stoica gave me the same look he had given Radu but without the head shake. At which point, I shut up.

"Are you making progress?" he said.

I stared back, questioning.

"Progress with your list," Stoica said.

That he knew about the list was maybe unnerving, maybe a little. But who was I kidding? It wasn't as if I had hidden what I was doing. I had pulled out the list in public, several times. I had dealt with at least three people, and Radu besides. It wasn't a secret because I hadn't wanted it to be a secret. It was my cover story, and it was backed up by a well-rehearsed legend, and it was OK that the Securitate knew because having them know the story and believe the story was how I was going to be allowed to remain in Bucharest.

That's what I kept telling myself, and I believed it in my head. My sphincter, though, was a different matter entirely.

"Some progress," I said, acknowledging the obvious. Playing dumb made no sense that that point.

"With how many?"

"A dozen or so?"

"And they've been released?"

"No, just identified," I said. "I know where they are. And I know the parameters of what it should take for the next step."

"Ah, the next step," Stoica said. With that, he offered a quick smile, as quick as a blink. I didn't know how to read it, the blink. I knew it was a euphemism for bribe money, and I assumed that he knew it was a euphemism for bribe money. What I couldn't tell was if that lightning smile was suggesting that Stoica wanted a piece of the bribe money or, perhaps, more than suggesting.

I took a deep breath, and then a long sip, and I tried to focus. He knew about the bribery scheme and didn't care, it seemed. That, I could understand. I had seen some of it in Hungary, too — the Soviets had people in high places in many/most of the government ministries, but the foot soldiers were locals. And in this situation, if you were a local, a Romanian, and the subject was Romanians who had been rounded up for a stint in a Ukrainian labor camp, well, it wasn't hard to see where your heart might lie.

Again, it was fairly predictable. And if Stoica had his hand out besides, well, I had seen that in Hungary, too. It was just human nature.

"I think I will have that drink now," he said, waving for Radu. "Two Manhattans. Rye for mine."

With that, we shared a companionable drink and discussed cocktails worth considering. Stoica dismissed the Old Fashioned with a wave of his hand and a "goddamn sugar water." He was much more of a thumbs-up on the gin and tonic: "A classic, and in this bar especially."

It went like that for 15 minutes or so, at which point Stoica stood up and reached for his wallet, and I said, "Please, let me," and he nodded a thank you and left without a word. And it was a good thing, too. If I had remained seated for even five more minutes, I probably would have soiled the barstool. Because while nothing about the encounter had been particularly surprising, it was still beyond unnerving. And I still didn't know if I was going to have to give Stoica a cut of the bribe money, or if the mere suggestion of it might insult him.

27

I took the tram about 10 stops. Like most of the trams and buses, there was a placard attached to each side. It said, "Long Live the Romanian People's Republic." The running joke, as people stood under the flimsy shelters and bitched about the inevitable delays, was, "Long Wait for the Romanian People's Republic."

I got out and walked the rest of the way to the train marshaling yard. Fritz had given me only two addresses before I left Vienna for Bucharest — for the Athenee Place and the marshaling yard. But I had put off my visit, just because. I really couldn't explain why, especially given just how much I wanted to get the fuck out of there.

"The good news is that there are a few ways out — really, only limited by your imagination," Fritz said.

"Pretend I have no imagination," I said.

"Won't need to."

"Won't need to what?"

"Won't need to pretend," Fritz said.

He laid out the escape routes in no particular order. What he called the "do it yourself" method was to simply cross the border from Romania into Hungary on my own.

"There's a million fucking ways in, which is the good news," Fritz said.

"And the bad news?"

"They've built up the border a lot in the last year, since the Communists. You might have to walk for miles, and there are plenty of watch towers and searchlights and barbed wire now. Oh, and the guards apparently have been offered bonuses based on how many they catch."

"Lovely," I said. "What else?"

"Going through Yugoslavia might be easier," Fritz said. "And we have a sherpa who can kind of guide you through. The problem is getting from there to Trieste. He offers some tips, but…"

"Great. And who is your sherpa. And do you cut him a check every month?"

"Rico."

"What the hell is a Rico?"

"Rico is the sherpa's name," Fritz said. "And, well, beats me. But he can be found at the only café in a dot of a place called Pojejena — it's just on the Romanian side of the border with Yugoslavia. Can you remember that?"

"Rico. Pojejena. Fuck me," I said.

"Yeah, well. The third way is probably the neatest and cleanest but it's also the riskiest, in some ways. We have a Russian…"

"Meaning?"

"We've paid him, just in case."

"So, just in case. Like, never been tested?"

"That's the risky part," Fritz said. "But he's taken our money, and it's really a pretty elegant solution. Romania has a minor trading relationship with Austria. Nobody on either side likes to talk about it but, well, we need some of their farm goods and they need Western currency — Swiss francs, in particular. So they ship us the wheat or whatever-the-hell in sealed trains that run from Bucharest, through Hungary, and straight to Vienna, and we pay for the shipment in Swiss francs — which they, in turn, use to buy Western goods."

"Because nobody wants their shitty money," I said.

"Exactly. But the point is, the train is sealed. Once the doors of the boxcars and closed and locked, they aren't opened until the train gets to Vienna. And that's you."

"Provided the Russian you have bribed stays bribed."

"Yes," Fritz said. "Provided."

The Russian was a sergeant. His name was Kirov. I asked for him at the guard shack, and a private pointed me toward a bigger hut a few hundred feet away. Kirov was inside, alone, feet on the desk.

"Sergeant Kirov?" I said.

"Who's asking?"

"Alex Kramer," I said, after sorting through my two identities and choosing my Athenee Palace name. I honestly wasn't sure why.

"Which means fuck-all to me," Kirov said.

At which point, I offered him the pass phrase. In the annals of stupid pass phrases, this was among the stupidest.

"Which do they hook up first, the locomotive or the caboose?"

To which Kirov offered the prearranged reply. Actually, there was no prearranged reply. He just said, "Goddamn idiotic, that. So, when do you want to go?"

"Not sure."

"Not helpful."

"Really, I'm not sure."

"Well, fine," he said. "It's really not a problem. Train runs Monday to Friday. Leaves at 5. You'd need to be here by 3."

"P.m., right?"

"No, 3 a.m."

"So 3 a.m. for a 5 a.m. train?"

"No, 3 a.m. for a 5 p.m. train."

"Why? Why so early?"

"Because," Kirov said, helpfully. "And it'll be just the one of you?"

"Yeah," I said, and then I thought about it. Would Sabina ever want to leave, despite what she said? Bogdan and Florin, maybe?

"What if it's more than one?"

"Just do the multiplication," Kirov said. "Two is $2,000. Three is $3,000."

"Do you have a maximum number?"

"Call it five — although it'll be a pretty tight squeeze, and how you'll all be able to have a piss without, well, I don't know."

It seemed easy enough. Kirov said he would give me an identification card, and that I should present it at the gate, and the guard would know what to do — he was in on it, among others. He said, "I mean, I only get a slice of the $1,000." I wanted to remind him about the money that the Gehlen Org had already paid him but let it go.

Kirov said that the 3 a.m. arrival would give them a chance to stash us in one of the boxcars being loaded overnight "with no bosses around." No luggage except maybe a knapsack would be permitted. And don't bother coming after 3 a.m., he said.

"Okay, repeat it all back to me," Kirov said, and I did. I got up to leave and said, "Okay, where's the identification card."

"Okay, where's the $1,000?"

"I have to pay in advance? What about the money you already got? And what if I don't—"

"Them's the rules," Kirov said. "You want in or not?"

"But I thought you were already paid—"

"Do you want in or not?"

I had brought the money, even though I hadn't expected to need it. After I handed over the $1,000, Kirov handed me a book of matches from some place called Long Legs."

"Subtle," I said.

"It's in Budapest. Or, was. I have fond memories."

"How long have you been here?"

"A year. Longest fucking year of my life."

"No long legs in Bucharest?"

"Only hairy legs," Kirov said.

"That's a shame," I said. I looked at the matchbook, saw the address on the back. I had spent some time in Budapest but didn't know the street even if I could imagine the place. Fond memories, yes.

"And this is all—" I said, holding up the matchbook.

"That's all you'll need," Kirov said.

I turned to leave and stopped.

"One question," I said.

"Shoot."

"Why are Russian soldiers in charge of the rail yard and not the locals?"

"Those fucking thieves?" Kirov said. And then, he laughed so hard that I thought he might hurt himself.

28

The walk from the Athenee Palace to the Romanian Athenaeum took two minutes, top. It was maybe 400 feet, door to door, from the best hotel in Bucharest to its most spectacular concert hall, an elaborate circular dome behind a rectangular entrance dominated by a row of columns. It was truly a beautiful building, and the word was that the acoustics and the appointments inside were just as spectacular. But, 400 feet. Or, as I repeated to myself a dozen times as I got dressed, "400 fucking feet."

Sabina had asked, begged, pleaded, and then insisted — and I kept putting her off until I couldn't anymore.

She would say, "But it's Mahler," and I kept giving her the full-philistine shrug.

And then she would say, "But it's the Fifth Symphony — I love the Fifth," and I kept telling her that I would buy her a fifth of whisky instead.

And then she would say, "My God, I hear the trumpets at the very beginning and I'm swept away, and the fourth movement, I swear, it makes me wet."

Then we had sex and I agreed. Which made me a male, I

guess, and her a female — but it didn't change the reality. That is, 400 feet — 400 fucking feet.

The problem was obvious. Sabina knew nothing about my life at the Athenee Palace, and nobody at the Athenee Palace knew anything about the part of my life where I blew up oil refineries and made the plans to do the self-same in the back room of The Dancing Waters while Sabina perched on a stool in the main room.

The collision of these two worlds could not happen. It would mean the end of whatever the hell I was trying to accomplish in Bucharest, and it would potentially put me in significant danger besides. I hadn't come close to having a problem in the weeks I had been there, but here I was, inviting one. Fritz would kill me if he knew — about Sabina, yes, but especially about the concert. I could hear him yelling, and the mantra I kept repeating myself might have been an attempt to drown him out — "400 fucking feet... 400 fucking feet..."

I left the hotel a half-hour early and walked in the opposite direction. There were a few people scattered around the lobby, and I could just tell that they were having a pre-concert drink before heading over. But I didn't recognize any of them and I was pretty sure none of them recognized me. If they did, well, I was just a face from the lobby. None of them knew my name or my story, and vice versa. If one of them happened to stumble into me in the Athenaeum's lobby before the concert and say something, I could just play dumb and suggest they were mistaken.

Still, left early and walked in the wrong direction a few blocks and then circled back for a different approach to the concert, just in case. When I arrived, Sabina was waiting next to one of the pillars that framed the entrance hall.

"Wet yet?" I said.

She punched me on the shoulder and said, "You'll see. You'll hear those trumpets and they'll grab you. By the fourth movement, you'll need to keep your program in your lap for camouflage."

As it turned out, the trumpets were just fine, thanks, and I didn't hate Mahler. Sabina and I held hands throughout. The best part was that it only lasted about 70 minutes. Then there was an intermission, followed by a Brahms something-or-other.

I said, "Do was have to stay for the Brahms bullshit?"

Sabina replied with another punch to the shoulder, and a "philistine," and then, "Let's have a drink and decide."

The intermission was like every intermission I had ever experienced, only maybe more. That is, the drinks were pre-mixed and lined up on trays behind several counters in the lobby area, and the men invariably were the ones queued up to carry two or three drinks back to the waiting women — one for her, two for him. I had no idea what was in the glasses, other than that it was alcohol that had undoubtedly been watered down by the management. It was my belief that the money from tickets paid the musicians while all of the profit for these concert halls was in the watered-down cocktails.

Anyway, it was after I paid my money and turned back toward where Sabina was waiting, and as I began to walk — slowly, triple-fisted — when I saw him on line at the next counter: Benny, the kid from the front desk.

He looked right at me. I swore he looked right at me. But there was nothing, no hint of recognition. There was no smile. There was no, "Good evening, Mr. Kramer, a fine evening it is." We weren't 20 feet apart, and he looked right at me, but nothing. Maybe it was as simple as seeing someone out of his regular context and not quite putting it together. It happens all the time. You're in a restaurant, and you see a face that you seem to recognize but can't quite remember how, and you dismiss it, not realizing until later that he's your mailman because the only place you've ever seen him before is in the lobby of your apartment.

So, maybe that was it. Or maybe it was something else. When I turned my head away, reflexively, I spotted a girl about Benny's age, beaming, wearing a pale pink dress with lace along the hem. She was about 10 feet behind me and must have been what Benny was looking at.

Still, however fortunate I had been, I couldn't rely on luck from there on. We needed to get the hell out of there — but in a way that didn't completely spook Sabina.

I handed her the drink and downed the first of mine in one.

"Thirsty, are we?" she said.

"Long line — I'm not sure how much time we have."

"A few minutes, certainly."

Sabina sipped, and I sipped. We were about 30 feet away from Benny and his date, and there were a dozen people between us, at least. I did my best to keep my back to them, which meant I had to subtly reposition Sabina. The look on her face indicated that she thought it a bit odd, but she appeared to buy it when I moved her and said, "That's better, out of the traffic flow."

She sipped, I sipped. She prattled on about the fourth movement, and I acted interested while trying to listen for what I was dreading, a shout from Benny, a "Mr. Kramer, Mr. Kramer..."

But, nothing. I looked around and realized I had one more problem. I had to assume that Benny and his girl had tickets upstairs, not in a box like Sabina and I. It was just a guess — for all I knew, some swell from the hotel had extra tickets and gave them to Benny — but I had to play the percentages, and the percentages told me that the front desk clerk could only afford the cheap seats. And, well, the stairs to the balcony were just to my right, which meant that if Benny and his girl took a straight line, they were going to brush my sleeve along the way. And if

Sabina and I headed to our box early, we would have to walk right past Benny.

I didn't know what to do.

Then the lobby lights blinked on and off.

"Time," Sabina said. All around us there was movement. I had no idea what to do, and so I fell back on the same street trick everyone used as part of their surveillance repertoire. I handed my drink to Sabina and said, "One second," and then I kneeled down to tie my shoe and said a prayer that getting out of Benny's line of site would work and not attract attention to me as he walked by.

One second, two seconds. Fritz is going to fucking kill me. Three seconds, four. He might even think I did it on purpose, just so I could manufacture a crisis that forced me to come home. Five seconds, six. I fumbled with the shoelace and held my breath. Then I saw it, the lace on the hem of the pale pink dress. It nearly brushed me as it went by but it didn't.

29

Bogdan and I were back in the insurance office that looked down on the back door of the Telephone Palace. We weren't supposed to be there but we wanted to watch the mission and neither of us could imagine the harm. The same guard let us in. He was surprised to see us but quickly recovered. Business was business, after all. We were prepared with some cash but, as it turned out, a bottle of rocket fuel was more than a sufficient inducement. He cradled it like a newborn and then walked us back up to the fifth floor.

We were a half-hour early, which meant killing time by bitching. Or, as I said more than once, "And explain to me exactly what the fuck sense this all makes?"

"You're preaching to the choir," Bogdan said.

"No, not that. I get the idea of the mission. What I don't understand is why one set of people does the surveillance and another set of people does the mission itself."

"Beats the shit out of me — but it's always been part of Constantin's way. Whenever I question it, he offers up some variation of 'many hands make work lighter,' or some such shit."

"But it makes no sense," I said.

"Well, at least the asshole is involved, and he was part of the surveillance," Bogdan said, and then he shrugged. And 15 minutes later, we pretty much said the same thing again.

Anyway, this time, the mission was being handled by Jake and Peter, the Yankee Odd Couple, along with Florin and Constantin. I had helped Peter prepare a dozen small explosive charges, just enough to damage the switchboard gizmos without trying to take down the structure of the building. It was supposed to be just bam-bam-bam, pow-pow-pow, and out. And Constantin figured that four of them would be enough to kill the two guards, especially since the guy outside would be taken by surprise and shot with a silenced pistol that Jake was carrying.

At two minutes before 2, Bogdan pointed down and said, "Showtime."

He was pointing at the four of them making their way down the side street, all wearing balaclavas and carrying weapons. Jake carried the silenced pistol, Constantin had a machine pistol that could fire a stream of rounds, Peter and Florin held rifles, and Peter had the explosive charges in a small pack on his back.

They were several hundred feet from the back door area. There, as before, the single guard was leaning against a stack of wooden crates and smoking a cigarette. His rifle, as before, was leaning up against the crates.

I looked back and forth, back and forth, as the four of them approached. At the corner, they were maybe 30 feet behind the stack of wooden crates. The guard was facing the other way. It was all as before.

Jake was in the lead, and the other three were behind him, single file. He held up his hand to signal a stop, and he waited maybe five seconds, then he dropped his hand and strode forward and turned to where he knew the guard would be, where the surveillance said he would be, and fired two silenced shots. The poor fucker died where he was, died with a lit cigarette in his hand.

The other three behind Jake arrayed themselves in such a way that all three would have a shot into the building when Jake pulled open the back door. In whatever position the guard at the desk happened to be — sitting, standing, reclining with his feet on the desk — one of the three would have a clear shot at him, and probably all three.

Jake grabbed the door handle with his left hand and motioned with the pistol in his right. One, two, three — and then he pulled open the door.

And then it all happened so fast. A barrage of gunfire met the opening of the door. There were at least three shooters inside, and probably more. They were clearly lying in wait.

I heard when Bogdan said, "Oh, fuck," and then he grabbed my arm. I remembered feeling it later, but maybe not at the time.

The initial blast of firing — it sounded like automatic weapons firing — cut down Jake as he was still holding the door handle. He looked as if he had been hit by dozens of bullets. There was no doubt that he was dead.

Then it all became a kind of kaleidoscopic haze. I saw snapshots after that more than a moving picture. I saw Constantin raise his machine pistol and take aim at the door — and then nothing. He slammed the weapon down and yelled "fuck" loud enough to be heard up in the insurance office.

So, there was him. And there was Peter, the farthest from the door, dropping his rifle and running away, the pack full of explosives bouncing up and down on his back.

And then there was Florin. He had dropped down to the ground to avoid the shooting. He dragged one of the wooden crates in front of him — fat lot of good it would do against a machine pistol — and perched his rifle on it and began firing and simultaneously waving at Constantin. He was providing cover fire, and Constantin paused for a second, hesitated, maybe shouted something. And then Florin waved more insistently and began firing again. With that — reluctantly, it seemed; again, there was an initial hesitation — Constantin then scampered off in the same direction that Peter had run.

With that it was Florin, alone.

"Come on, brother," Bogdan said, more to himself than to me.

Florin kept firing into the door, intermittently. He would fire, and inch his way backward a couple of feet, dragging the wooden crate along with him. He would fire again, and repeat the same maneuver. There was no more firing from inside. It wasn't likely that Florin had killed them all. They were just reacting to the shots and taking cover. Once, twice, then a third time. Back, back, back Florin crept. One more and he might be far enough back to make a run for it by using the stack of wooden crates as cover.

One more.

Then Bogdan and I heard the empty click.

"Shit" is all both of us could manage, pretty much simultaneously. Click. Florin was out of ammunition. There would be nothing to prevent the guards inside from firing now, and Florin would have to make a run for it, come what may. And he might have made it, too, if three more guards from inside the building that was supposed to have only one inside guard came around the corner from the same direction that our guys had arrived. They came up behind Florin and could have killed him on the spot. Instead, they arrested him.

I guess that was when I really felt Bogdan squeezing my arm. There would be marks there the next day, bruises in the outline of his fingers, the first two and the thumb.

30

The prearranged follow-up meeting after the Telephone Palace mission was set for about 40 hours after the completion of the operation — up on Metropolitan Hill at 8 p.m. on the night after the night after. By my rough calculation, Bogdan and I spent about 30 of those 40 hours drinking.

At first, he said, he needed the fortification before going to tell his parents about Florin, which necessitated him telling them about the anti-Communist commando squad to which they were attached. I actually went with him — it was an hour's walk, easily — and sat outside on the curb. When Bogdan eventually came out, I clearly heard his mother wailing when the door opened.

After that, fortification morphed into attempted sedation. We drank and replayed what we had witnessed from the window of the insurance company. We drank and cursed Peter's cowardice because one more rifle would have made a difference, perhaps all the difference. We drank and wondered where all the extra guards inside the Telephone Palace had come from, contradicting both Constantin's intelligence and our two nights of surveillance. We drank and worried about Florin most of all. Meanwhile, the sum total of our expressions of regret toward Jake amounted to two statements:

"Poor fucker," I said.

"Poor asshole," Bogdan said.

We drank all of that next day in whatever bar would have us — all of that next day and all of that next night. I imagine that we ate something at some point but I couldn't be positive. The sun was coming up when I finally managed to push Bogdan into his apartment and I headed to the rooming house.

I crept in as quietly as I could manage, but I was cooked and kind of pinballed from handrail to handrail as I made my way up the stairs. Ion heard me and came out of his apartment.

"Christ, don't light a match," he said.

I shrugged and fiddled with my key in the lock.

"Here," Ion said, taking the key from me. He handed it back to me after the door was open.

"If I smell puke soaked into the bed the next time I'm in here, it's coming out of your deposit," he said.

Whatever. I set the alarm for 4 p.m., which would give me about eight hours to recover. I passed out with my clothes on and the little clock resting on my chest. When it rang, I was still drunk but at least functional. A bath brought me back a few measures farther, and so did some coffee made on my hotplate.

I held out my hand, and it shook only a little, and that was going to have to be good enough because I needed to send a message to Fritz. I wrote it down, and then tightened it by at least a third. Then I translated it using the cipher book, a copy of *Little Women*, of all things. We were up to page 78, and the key was simple: if I sent the number 3, it corresponded to the third letter on page 78. If you didn't know the book or the page, you couldn't crack the code. After that, I pulled the radio out from between the mattress and the box spring and sent what I had —

the news that the mission had imploded, and that Jake was dead, and that Constantin's machine pistol had jammed, and that Peter the coward had run, and that Florin had been arrested, and that there had been an overall intelligence failure of quite a magnitude.

Fritz's reply, after several minutes:

"Your role?"

I didn't see the harm in admitting the truth.

I sent, "Observed clandestinely from a distance with Bogdan. Unauthorized."

Fritz's reply:

"Foggy."

For the first time, I really did feel like throwing up. Foggy. That was the one code word that Fritz and I had worked out ahead of time. It was a signal to me that the intelligence I had provided did not match up to what Fritz and the Gehlen Organization had been told by the Americans. In the two previous missions, there had been no discrepancies. Whatever I saw and reported back was whatever the Americans apparently saw and reported back. The whole thing had been pretty smooth and uneventful. Now, though, foggy. Christ.

It had been a day and a half, after all, so it wasn't out of the question that the Americans would have received word before I sent my message to Fritz — received it from Peter, presumably, seeing as how Jake was now among the dearly departed. That he would have tried to cover his own ass made some sense, which would potentially lead to him altering the truth in his report to his bosses. And if that was the sum total of the reason for "foggy," well, fine.

I had no idea, though, and really no way of finding out. Because "foggy" not only meant that there was a discrepancy. It also meant a combination of "watch your back" and "nothing for at least 48 hours" — the thought being that a little time might allow the fog to lift, and that there was no sense trying to figure out anything else in the meantime. Which sounded idiotic in the moment — but it was what Fritz and I had agreed before I got on the train in Vienna.

Foggy, then. And it wasn't my imagination — my hand was shaking worse than before I sent the message.

PART III

31

Bogdan and I went to the meeting together. The streets were quiet — or, quiet-ish — and the weather was benign. The easy walk up to Metropolitan Hill would have pleasant under many circumstance but not these.

We began with an argument.

"We can't tell them that we watched the whole thing," I said.

"Why not?"

"Because we can't. Because it was against the fucking rules."

"Fuck the rules. We saw it."

"And now we pretend we didn't," I said. "I mean, what does it matter? Just play dumb."

"And how do I explain knowing about Florin?"

"You don't explain because you don't know."

"That's fucking stupid — of course, I know."

"It's not stupid," I said. "I mean, you know he didn't come home. You realized it the next morning. So, you tell them you went to your parents' house, and they didn't know anything. And then you say you went to the new girlfriend's place, and she didn't know anything. That's when you started getting worried and came to my place. And then we were stuck because we didn't know how to contact anybody else — so we went to The Dancing Waters, but nobody was there, and that was that."

"I don't know."

"It works," I said. "It holds together just fine. You're worried about your brother but you don't know the truth. I'm telling you, it's better this way. No sense starting World War III — it's already fucked up enough."

"All right, all right," Bogdan said. Then, after 10 or 15 more steps: "Alex, I mean, I can't fucking think straight. I just keep thinking of Florin in the system and... fuck."

I really didn't know anything about "the system," other than what Jake had told me that night in the bar where the brainwashed guy wandered in for a beer and then wandered out again. I'm not even sure I believed it, what Jake said. Not until Bogdan sat down on the curb and just started babbling. The system. The system.

"It's a fucking nightmare — you don't get it, I don't think," he said. "If he gets put in the system, he probably doesn't come out. And if he does come out, he'll be a goddamned vegetable."

"So, the brainwashing..."

"So, you've heard about that. Good. It's all fucking true. And Florin, Christ, you know him. He's a sweet kid. If they drag his ass into Pitesti..."

"What's that, Pitesti?"

"The brainwashing prison," Bogdan said, and then he started crying. I didn't know what to do, so I just watched him sob until he wiped his nose on his sleeve and started talking again.

"Pitesti," he said. "Some people have gotten out, and some stories have been told, and part of you thinks it's bullshit, but why would anybody make it up? I mean, just fucking horrible stories. There was a guy who tried to slash his wrists, and then he broke up the razor blade and swallowed the pieces to keep the guards from finding out who gave it to him. But the guy lived, and they pulled the fragments out of his shit and examined them for fingerprints. Nothing, apparently."

"Good to know," I said, trying to lighten the mood by even a milligram. And, well, it was maybe a half-milligram.

"There was this guy named Pintilie — just a brutal animal, an officer. I don't know if he was in Pitesti or not, but everybody tells stories about him. He supposedly beat some guy to death with an iron bar and then, just for laughs, tied a bunch of stones around the mother of the dead guy and tossed her into the Cris."

"Where's that?"

"A river in Transylvania," he said. "And there's another guy, Nicolski. He once beat a woman senseless with a leather hose filled with sand, then banged her head against the wall, then knocked out all but six of her teeth."

"Jesus."

"Yeah, that's who they are. And Pitesti, it's their crown jewel. They take people there to brainwash them. They try to turn the anti-Communists into Communists. They try to take the religious people and suck the religion out of them. One of the stories is that they make them recite their prayers, except they have to substitute curses for the holy words. Instead of Holy Communion, they make them eat wafers of shit. They beat them, half drown them, make them sleep with the lights on, sleep standing up, just try to break them, do it until they do it — or until they kill them trying. They call it 'unmasking.'"

Bogdan stopped again, sobbed again. I let him go for about 30 seconds, then looked at my watch and stood.

"We're going to be late," I said.

We walked and Bogdan did his best to pull himself together. I looked at him, and snot stained both of his sleeves, but no one else was likely to notice. We got to the top of Metropolitan Hill and walked into the complex. Over by the chapel, we could see

Valentina next to Peter, and then Constantin walked out of the chapel and toward the bench.

"Shit," Bogdan said.

"What?"

"I mean, I knew Florin wasn't going to be there but, still..."

"I know, I know. Just remember, we don't know anything."

"Yeah, yeah," Bogdan said, and then he looked at me.

"But what if he's already in Pitesti?" he said.

32

"Where's Florin?" Bogdan said.

"Where's Jake?" I said.

Peter looked at his shoes. Valentina stared off into the distance. Constantin hesitated.

"Is somebody going to fucking tell us?" Bogdan said, and then he went through what we had talked about, all in a breathless burst — worrying when Florin didn't show up the next morning, then seeing his parents, then seeing the girlfriend, then going to The Dancing Waters. He spit it out in about ten angry seconds. It was a hell of a ten seconds of acting.

"So, where the fuck is he?" Bogdan said.

Constantin cleared his throat.

"Jake is dead, and Florin was arrested," he said.

Bogdan wiped a tear. Not acting, not anymore.

"How the fuck..." I said.

Constantin looked at Valentina. Peter continued to look at his shoes.

"It was fucking Jake," Constantin said. "Fucking cowboy."

Bogdan seemed frozen. I looked at Constantin and shrugged.

"What? How?" I said. "Two guards, four of you. What the hell?"

"More than two guards," Constantin said. I could barely hear him.

"But how?" I said. "I mean, we saw two, only two. First night, second night, only two."

"We could have handled it," Constantin said. "I don't know why it was more, but we could have handled it. We could have, but fucking Jake..."

With that, Constantin stopped and seemed to be gathering his thoughts. What we had seen from our perch in the insurance office was Jake opening the back door and getting slaughtered. What Constantin said, after his pause, was different. He said that the outside guard went according to plan — but that Jake rushed to the back door and exposed himself before the rest of them were in position to support him.

"If he waits for my signal..." Constantin said. I did my best at that point to keep my eyes on Constantin and not look over at Bogdan because, if his memory was like my memory, Jake didn't reach for the door handle until the other three were in position and until he gave them a countdown with the raised hand that held his pistol. One, two, three.

"And then, my machine pistol jammed," Constantin said. Bogdan let out a small cry.

"Peter was never in a position to do anything because Jake had rushed the door — so I ordered him to hoof it. Then Florin, he did what he could, giving me cover to get away while he fired, but then he ran out of ammunition and..."

"Motherfuckers," Bogdan said.

Everybody went silent after that. I didn't know what the rest of them were thinking but I was desperately trying to understand the inconsistencies between what we saw and what Constantin said. Other than the business about Jake going off-script, the rest of the story resembled the truth, kind of. The bit about him ordering Peter to run away — that was bullshit, but fine. He was just protecting the kid. The part about the machine pistol jamming and Florin offering cover fire for Constantin to escape — that was all consistent with what Bogdan and I had seen.

But the cowboy business? The not being in position to support him business? All bullshit. But why? Was it as simple as Constantin covering his own ass for a faulty plan?

I would spend hours thinking about that in the days after. But then and there, on the benches on Metropolitan Hill, there was too much information in my head and not nearly enough time to process it. At some point, I turned and looked at Bogdan, and he was borderline catatonic.

He stayed that way, too, until a blurted out, "So, what about Florin?"

"What about him?" Valentina said. Her first words.

"What the fuck about Florin?" I said.

"Calm down," Constantin said.

"The hell I will," I said, and now Bogdan was on his feet, the only one, his angry presence now looming over the rest of us.

"Fucking right," he said.

Constantin looked at Valentina, and then the two of them stared at the two of us. Cold fury was what I felt.

"We can't just leave him there," I said, a little more quietly. But I stood up, too.

Valentina said, "Don't be naive, Alex. What are we supposed to do, storm the gates? Be realistic. This isn't some fantasy story. There's only four of us. And besides, we don't even know where he is, not for sure."

"You fucking disgust me," I said.

"Easy now," Constantin said. "Everybody sit down and calm down."

33

"Alex, be reasonable," Constantin said.

"Bogdan's brother — our fucking brother — has been arrested. There's nothing reasonable about it. There's an obligation.

"There's no obligation to commit suicide," Valentina said.

"There's an obligation to try, and if you can't fucking see that..."

"Enough," Constantin said.

"You're not going to shut me up," I said. "I've been doing this for almost as long as you've been fucking alive — and you don't leave your brother on the field. You don't abandon him. You have to fucking try."

Bogdan's eyes were bulging out, and he seemed ready to explode. I put my hand on his shoulder, and he looked at me, and settled down just a bit. I doubt that he understood it, but he seemed willing to follow my lead. And the truth was, if this turned into a hysterical plea from Bogdan to save his flesh-and-blood brother, it would end up being a waste of time.

"We have to fucking try," I said.

"We don't know where he is." Valentina, again.

"Take a guess."

Constantin and Valentin looked at each other and mumbled one word simultaneously: "Jilava."

"Tell me about Jilava," I said.

Constantin explained that it was a local prison — "more of a jail than a prison, I guess," he said. "South of town."

"How far?"

"I don't know, seven or eight miles," he said. Then he looked at Valentina for confirmation, and she nodded.

"Seven," she said.

"Like I said, more of a jail," Constantin said. "From what we know, it's kind of a holding place. When you're there, you're really not in the system. They don't just have political prisoners there — it's all kinds of prisoners. But the political prisoners arrested around here, that's where they go before they get transferred into the gulag. It's like a way station, a jail where you get processed."

"Has anybody seen the setup?" I said.

Constantin and Valentin shook their heads. Peter continued to look at his shoes. Fucking coward. Bogdan said, "I've seen it."

"When?" Constantin said.

"When I was a kid — you know, in school. Just me and a couple of buddies, fucking around. You know, before the Commies."

"What do you remember?"

"Not much. A gate out front — we got shooed away by the guards there."

"Big fence?"

"Kind of a shitty fence — just like a fence around a playground," Bogdan said.

"And the prison itself?"

"I don't know."

"Try," I said.

"I don't know — stone walls, some kind of entrance in front, small parking lot — I remember that because one of my buddies tried to hit a parked truck with an apple core."

"Did he come close?"

"Close enough."

"So, not much distance between the gate and the parked cars — good, good," I said.

I probed at Bogdan's memory but he didn't have anything else worthwhile. I turned back to Constantin.

"How long?" I said.

"How long what?"

"How long before Florin gets transferred into the system?"

"There's no way to know."

"Take a guess. Your best guess."

"Days, probably," Constantin said. "Three, four days."

"And this is Day 2," I said.

Then I took a deep breath and reiterated the main point: that we had to try. Constantin talked about three problems: "no military-style vehicle, no weapons other than pistols and one rifle, and biggest of all, not enough people. Look around. We're it — and while it might only be a jail, it's not like it's unguarded. I'm sure it's fucking crawling with guards. One look at us — one, two, three, four, five."

"More like about three and a half," I said, staring directly at Valentina. I would have stared at Peter, but he still hadn't looked up.

Constantin looked at me, and his eyes told me to knock it off. So, I did.

"We need a truck that looks kind of military, or even a big car," I said. "We only need two of us — me and Bogdan. He can get by with a pistol and I'll take the rifle, and that's it."

"You're going to bust Florin out of prison with a goddamned popgun?" Constantin said.

I nodded, and started to explain. But there was one more interruption.

"But what if he isn't there?"

Valentina, again.

34

Christ, what was her name? It had only been seven years, and sometimes it seemed like 70, but that was no excuse. Seven years: Limoges to Paris to Normandy to Vienna to Innsbruck to Istanbul to Budapest to Tallinn to Bucharest — and with a dozen other places in between. Seventy? More like 700.

Clarisse. Clarisse Morean. Of course. Clarisse.

It was in Limoges. It was during the worst months of my life, the months after Manon's tiny airplane disappeared after fleeing the Gestapo in Lyon. I should have been on the plane with her. There should never have been a plane, not if the planning had been better. The what-ifs filled my hours, waking and sleeping. What if. What if.

I felt guilty and grief-stricken at once, a malevolent stew of emotions that I couldn't shake. I was angry and bitter and ruthless beyond reason when it came to the Germans — vengeful, reckless, all of that. Leon and I were attached to a group of maquis in the hills outside of Limoges — and the two of us, the best of friends, weren't getting along, either.

And there was Clarisse. She was a teacher from the city who

rode out to the hills on her bicycle to act as a combination big sister/foster mother for the young guys in our group — counseling, consoling, delivering mail to their sweethearts, whatever. I forgot how young some of them were — 17, 18, 21 — and that they had never been away from home. They were brave as hell during the daylight hours, but less so after the sun went down, especially after they had been drinking. Clarisse talked them down when she visited, listened to them, advised them, comforted them. And the two of us, for a brief time — a blink, really — became lovers.

Clarisse. She would never leave Limoges — because that's where he people were, her job, her life. She would never leave and I would never stay — because I had no people left, no one except Leon, and he was determined to get to Paris and fight there for the Resistance. We were destined to separate — that much, we both knew in our hearts. So, a blink.

But then it happened. I demanded vengeance when one of our group of maquis was taken and killed. I demanded it, and I got it with some assistance. A man from the Free Guard was our victim. His death, well, we drunkenly celebrated it — until, that is, we got the news. Because the Germans typically demanded retribution of their own in such situations. They often demanded 100 French deaths for every one of theirs. They typically emptied the jails of drunks and petty criminals to reach the quota — and it was understood by everyone on both sides as the cost of doing business.

Understood. Accepted, even. Until we received the news that back in Limoges, in the hours after our vindication, the hours when we were celebrating, a woman with a flat tire was picked up for a curfew violation and deposited in this old city jail, the maison d'arrêt.

A woman: Clarisse. Clarisse Morean.

"The time frame was about the same, about 72 hours," I said.

I was explaining it all to Constantin and the rest. They were hanging now on every word, less skeptical than in my thrall.

"The Germans were very precise that way, on the off chance that they managed to catch the people who killed their guy. They announced it on all the handbills that they pasted to the walls. If they hadn't made an arrest in 72 hours, they would kill 100 French citizens. They just advertised the fact."

"And?" Valentina, again.

"And we got her out, me and another guy," I said. I didn't mention Leon's name because, well, it wouldn't have meant anything to them.

"I don't know, some little city jail — I have to think Jilava is bigger than that, more substantial," Constantin said.

"You have a better fucking idea?" I said.

"I mean, just go in blasting?" he said.

"Are you suicidal?" Valentina said.

"I'm not suicidal, and nobody said anything about going in blasting," I said. At that point, I explained how it went down and how I was able to walk Clarisse out of the jail without a shot being fired, without a weapon so much as being drawn.

"I don't know, it sounds like luck to me," Constantin said.

"That's talking bullshit."

"Long shot at best," Valentina said.

"Even money at worst," I said.

"Now who's talking bullshit?" she said.

Peter still had not looked up. Bogdan had not stopped looking at me with a face that was all hope and trust. It made me feel a little uncomfortable, to be honest. I mean, I was glad he trusted my judgment — but Valentina wasn't completely wrong. It probably was somewhere between even money and a long shot, probably closer to a long shot, probably something like 70-30 against. It was different from Limoges. Jilava probably was a bigger jail with more elaborate security procedures. I had spent time in Limoges, knew a few people in Limoges. And while I had lived in Bucharest for several weeks, it was just... different. There were so many things I didn't know.

"But what's the alternative?" I said. I was talking to both of them but looking squarely at Constantin. Valentina was hopeless and, really, not worth the bother. This would be his call in the end. Of that, I was certain.

"You want us to walk away because it's risky. Well, no. I will not be a coward — I'll fucking do it without you if I have to, me and Bogdan. But it isn't suicide, despite what you think. It has worked before and I really believe it can work again."

"Limoges and Bucharest are very different places," Valentina said.

"But soldiers are soldiers, and bureaucracies are bureaucracies, and that's what I'm counting on."

I went on to explain the plan in more detail, and they listened to what I was saying, and their faces did not suggest outright rejection. Well, Constantin's didn't.

"It'll just be me and Bogdan — no backup, no need for a backup," I said. "A backup would only complicate things, and maybe fuck them up. Just the two of us. Just me and Bogdan. We need two uniforms and a vehicle that looks like it's military — or, whatever. Not necessarily military, just bulky. Black and bulky. Not a roadster. We need that, and we need a forger to work up the letterhead. We can do that, right?"

"We have the uniforms already," Constantin said.

"And the forger?"

Constantin nodded.

"Where?"

"The tea house where I took you," he said. "Day after tomorrow, 2 p.m."

"Day after tomorrow? That's too fucking late."

"Might be, might not."

"Why not quicker? Why not tomorrow morning?"

"Best I can do is 2 p.m., day after tomorrow."

"But that's Day 4."

"What part of 'best I can do' don't you understand?" Constantin said.

"But why?"

"You've met the forger. He's my cousin. And he's away at his in-laws until the day after tomorrow."

"It's too late."

"Maybe not."

"Christ."

"Like I said, best I can do," Constantin said.

I looked over at Valentina. She started to say something but I interrupted her before she could.

"I know, I know, 'And what if he isn't in there?'" I said, half mimicking her voice. "Well, if he isn't in there, we've still learned something. We'll know where he isn't, and maybe where he is, and if we have that information, we can decide about next steps."

She shook her head but said nothing, because she knew what I knew — that Constantin had already agreed to help.

35

With time to kill — every bit of a day and a half — I stopped by Sabina's apartment. I knew she was off, but she didn't want to stay in. I had no idea what to do — I was thinking a couple of drinks, followed by sex and a quick exit — but she wanted to walk. So, walk we did — far out along one of the main streets, out to the Triumphal Arch. There were a bunch of mansions along the way, although I had no idea if the swells still lived in them, seeing as how the Communists who currently ran the country were decidedly anti-swell.

For what it was worth, I didn't see a single light on in any of them. What I did see, though, was a billboard. Big and all lit up. The picture was of Uncle Sam with green claws, holding a bag of money, and there was a Romanian worker with a shield fending him off. The words at the bottom: "Never shall we yield to imperialism."

And, well, whatever. Five minutes past the billboard, we reached our destination.

"Well, what do you think?" she said.

What I wanted to tell her was that it looked like what would result if the Arc de Triomphe in Paris took a shit. A baby Arc de Triomphe.

"Cute?" I said.

"Oh, you've seen the real one."

I nodded.

"You know, they like to refer to Bucharest as 'Little Paris,'" she said.

I didn't know how to react to that one. I said, "I guess I can see it," but I really couldn't.

There was a café on the corner of one of the streets leading to the arch. We chose a table where both of us could look at it from where we sat. It was night, and there wasn't much traffic, and they did have the thing lit up, and it did stand out and kind of glimmer in the darkness. But, no.

"What's wrong?" Sabina said, after the waiter had brought the wine. Red. Shit.

I couldn't tell her about the botched operation at the Telephone Palace, and about Florin being captured, and about my scheme to get him out of Jilava. It was all I could think about, though. I mean, I trusted her because, well, because she was at least adjacent to our little group. She allowed us to use the back room at The Dancing Waters, and there was a risk in that for her, and that wasn't nothing. But still. If my years in the Resistance had taught me anything, it was compartmentalization. The left hand did not have to know what the right hand was doing — in fact, it was better if it didn't. Every mission was need-to-know, and she didn't need to know.

Still, we had become close enough that she knew something was on my mind. I had to say something, and I did what I had been trained to do: change the subject and revert to a safer truth. It wasn't hard.

"It's just the whole 'Little Paris' thing," I said. "Little Paris reminds me of Big Paris, and Big Paris is a place where I have tried, well, I've tried to leave a lot of my memories behind."

I wasn't sure if I had told her about my time in the Resistance. I had, obviously, because I told her about Manon — but I wasn't sure about the rest of my time, especially the Paris time.

We both sipped. She touched my hand.

"I have memories here, too," Sabina said. "I have memories that I would like to, as you say, leave behind. But I can't because to leave the memories would mean leaving Bucharest, and I just can't. I love it so."

"I just don't get it. You love a place that, if you hadn't been able to disguise your past, would have shoved you into a boxcar on a train and had you killed at the other end."

"That was the Nazis, not Bucharest."

"You keep telling yourself that," I said. "But you know, deep down, what the average Gentile in Bucharest thought. They were happy not to know about the boxcars. They would swear on a stack of their fucking Bibles that they didn't know. But, well, really? What did they think when the house next door went empty, when they heard the black cars pull up and the banging on the door in the middle of the night? Like they didn't know? Stack of fucking Bibles."

"It's more... complicated than that," she said. It was almost a whisper.

"Not so complicated."

"You weren't here then."

"But I was alive then," I said.

Pause. Drink.

"I mean, fuck," I said.

Pause. Drink.

"You'll never understand," Sabina said.

Pause. Drink.

"I understand what my life in Paris was," I said. "And I

understand that, when the shooting stopped, there was no way I could stay there. I did good things there — heroic, even if I do say so myself."

"If you do say so yourself," Sabina said. Then, she smiled and I smiled back.

"But war, it changes you," I said. "Heroic, yes — but ruthless, too. Just fucking ruthless. And if I could justify pretty much everything I did — and I could — and if I could look in the mirror when it was over, well, let's just say I couldn't look for too long. I couldn't and I didn't want to. The shit was just too real."

"You can't ignore reality," she said, quietly.

"I can try."

"To what end?"

I had no answer for that one. We drank up, and walked back to Sabina's place, and had the sex that I had been angling for when I first arrived. She offered me the other side of her bed for the rest of the night but I begged off, mostly because I wasn't likely to sleep very much. The conversation and the sex had been a welcome diversion, but the thoughts about the Telephone Palace and Florin and Jilava were all front-and-center again. I wanted a shower and clean sheets back at the Athenee Palace, but settled on the rooming house. It was closer, and I was exhausted.

It was only later, much later, when I found out about the man who was waiting in the shadows outside of Sabina's apartment building, the man who was following me as I trudged through the night.

36

There was nothing to do but keep going. Two names, two missions, two places of residence, and still more than a day to kill before the meeting with the forger. Keep going. Keep going.

After a long sleep at the rooming house, I did get my shower at the Athenee Palace. That was after Benny, the kid from the front desk, chased me to the elevator with a message that had been delivered the previous day.

"Sorry I missed you," he said.

"No worries," I said.

He smiled like he knew something. I smiled like I didn't have a care in the world, like I hadn't missed a night at the hotel. Anyway, the note was from my still-unnamed agent in the business of identifying the names on my list. The meeting he sought was for 2 p.m. in the English Bar.

I arrived just before 2, and Radu was just coming on duty.

"I've missed you," he said.

"Been busy."

"Yes, yes, busy."

My contact was late, and I was well into my second Manhattan when he arrived. The English Bar did a kind of free lunch sometimes, and Radu had brought me a plate of pickles and cured meats that appeared to have seen better days. Still, I was picking away at the pile when my guy showed up.

He barely put his ass on the stool when I said, "You've been fucking me, asshole."

The guy looked shocked.

"The Securitate," I said. "You couldn't keep your fucking mouth shut, could you?"

"I haven't said a word."

"Bullshit."

"Not a word."

"Then what is the man in the black suit doing, sitting on that very stool, knowing all about my list?"

He stuttered, then stopped, then stuttered again.

"How the hell am I supposed to be able to trust you?" I said. "We're supposed to be partners in this. I already gave you the goddamned money. I trusted you, and now this, this, this shit."

Radu was on the periphery, waiting for a pause to bring the guy's drink. It took him about five seconds to swoop in, set it down, and swoop out.

"I didn't say a fucking word," is what he finally said. "To the Securitate? Not a word. Not one. Are you kidding me — it could be my head, too."

"Then how?"

"How? You're a foreigner staying at the Athenee. If your room isn't bugged, it's an oversight. If your trash isn't being emptied on some desk in headquarters every day, emptied and picked through, it's because somebody is on vacation."

"Nothing in my trash but used tissues."

"The point is, they've likely been tracking you since you stepped off the train. You're naive if you think otherwise."

"I'm not naive."

"You sure fucking sound it," he said, and then he took the first sip of his drink, a big sip.

I knew he was probably right, but I had to go full-indignant on him. I had to gauge his reaction, if nothing else. My partner here, while he clearly wasn't a virgin when it came to the business of bureaucratic chiseling, well, I'm not sure he had quite turned pro, either. If there were cracks — in his story, his facade, his demeanor — they might show at a time of stress. And while I wasn't an expert or anything on this kind of thing, I mean, I did have eyes and instincts — and they told me that the guy was as advertised. That is, he was as worried about the Securitate as I was.

We drank some more in silence until I said, "So?"

"So, what?"

"So, why are we meeting? You left the message."

"It's about that extra name you gave me," he said, and then his eyes dropped down to his hands but just for a blink.

"What about him?"

"What's his name again?"

I had to think for a second before I remembered, "Mikhal Popescu." Sofia's husband, Mikhal. And then, I wondered about why I didn't take her back to one of those railroad hotels across from the station. Just for a blink, though. Half a blink.

"Well, there's no way," he said.

"And exactly what does that mean?"

"No way. Too hot."

"What the fuck does that mean?"

"What I said — too hot."

"What if I upped the price?" I said, figuring that this was just more negotiating.

"It's not the money."

"Then what?"

"What part of 'too hot' don't you understand?" he said.

I nodded across the bar at Radu, and he brought us reinforcements. I asked him if there was anything else for lunch, and he produced a few slices of the blackest bread I had ever seen along with some cheese slices that were even less appetizing than the meat.

Whatever. My partner inhaled the platter, and we sat and drank in companionable silence for the most part. And two drinks became three, and then three drinks became four.

I waved at Radu for another, but my partner grabbed my arm and shook his head. He was half falling off of the stool as it was. As he tried to stand, well, let's just say that it took him resting both hands on the bar to accomplish such a herculean feat.

"Wait a minute," I said.

He reached into his pocket and said, "Sorry."

"No, not the bill. You have to tell me about 'too hot.' What in the actual fuck is 'too hot'? I have to know. It's important that I understand."

He stood there, both hands on the bar, and I thought his knees were going to buckle for a second. When he leaned over, apparently to whisper in my ear, he lost his balance and I had to steady him by placing a hand on each of his shoulders.

"I shouldn't," he said.

"I need to know."

"Okay, okay."

I took my hands back, and he was steady.

"The Securitate," he said.

"What about it?"

"Your guy?"

"What about him?"

"He's Securitate," he said. "He's on some kind of assignment."

"But..."

"All I have," the guy said, and he began walking away. Then he stopped and said, "And don't ask me for anything more, because there isn't enough money in the world for me to ask any more questions about your fucking Mikhal Popescu."

37

I needed a nap and was headed from the English Bar to the elevator — and handling the half-flight of steps down to the lobby just fine, thank you — when I felt two hands grabbing my elbows from behind. Two hands, two men, two black suits. As it turned out, the ride to Securitate headquarters on a street named after someone named Demetru I. Dobrescu didn't take 10 minutes.

Part of me couldn't think entirely straight because of the five Manhattans — yes, I did have the fifth after my guy left the bar. The other part wondered if I had really been that wrong about what I had just witnessed in the bar. My partner was not Securitate, and every ounce of intuition that I possessed told me that he was just as afraid of them as I was. But, well, here I was in the back of the big black car.

I had seen these kinds of places before, too many times. The cells were always in the basement, the cells where the bad shit took place. I always got this involuntary shiver when I thought about it because the thought inevitably took me to probably my greatest fear. That is, torture performed by attaching one end of the wires to an electrical current with the other ends clipped to my balls. I had seen the apparatus but never suffered the experience — and the fear of it might have been somehow worse than the reality. Anyway, I always got a shiver when I thought about it. Always.

If this was like all the others, the cells would be in the basement and the offices would be on the upper floors. Nazis in Germany, Arrow Cross in Hungary, Soviets in Tallinn — didn't matter. It was always the same. And so, it was with a sense of relief as I began to climb the stairs at No. 5 Demetru I. Dobrescu, to climb up to the third floor with the assistance of the two black suits, one per elbow.

Third office down on the left. Door open. Captain Mihai Stoica behind the desk, filling in some kind of ledger.

"Ah, Mr. Alex Kramer, I'm so glad you could join me," he said, motioning toward the empty wing chair across from his desk. The two black suits left and closed the door behind them.

"Your friends are most efficient and persuasive."

"Yes, yes they are," Stoica said. He chuckled and wrote down one more entry in the ledger before blotting it and closing the book with a thwack that he seemed to enjoy.

"Now, then," he said, reaching into a desk drawer and removing a red cardboard file. He opened the file and slowly turned over pages — three, four, maybe five.

"We've been busy," he said. "So many men here. Busy, yes, verifying bits of your story."

He looked like he thought of something suddenly, and he looked back down at the pile of papers and turned back to the second or third sheet. He scanned it with the assistance of his right index finger, tracing down until he found what he was looking for and then tapping the sheet. If the purpose was to frighten me, he was doing a hell of a job.

"Here's what I can't figure — can you help me with this," Stoica said.

"If I can," I said, my voice breaking like a 14-year-old's. Stoica smiled at my discomfort. And if I was showing how scared I was — and I was showing it — I knew that the fear could work in my favor. The last thing I wanted to do was appear to be a cool professional. Much better, in this circumstance, to piss down my leg — metaphorically if not actually.

"So, here's the thing," Stoica said. "I go 'round and 'round on this and can't quite satisfy myself."

He paused. I held my breath.

"It's your motivation," he said. "You and your list and the money you're spending — why? What do you get out of it?"

"To help people."

"No financial reason? Just pure charity."

I nodded.

"Really?"

I took a deep breath and decided to tell him the fiction I had told my partner, the bit about my father, and how he had taken advantage of half of the town, and how I wanted to make amends.

"My name is shit in that town," I said. "With this, maybe..."

I let it hang there. Stoica's eyes locked onto mine — three, four, five seconds. Maybe more. Then he broke first, returning to the red folder on his desk.

He exhaled loudly.

"It seems odd, your release," he said.

"Release?"

"From the Ukrainian work camp."

"Odd how?"

"No paperwork."

"No offense, but I have no idea about the paperwork," I said. "All I know is, I'm fucking here."

Another sigh. He turned another page.

"Tell me about the camp," Stoica said.

This one, I felt I could handle. Fritz and the Gehlen people had debriefed the real Alex Kramer after they got him out of the camp and into his new life in Cologne. They had anticipated this potential line of questioning and had elicited all manner of detail about the work camp. In between the Romanian language records and the rest, I had been repeatedly quizzed about these details. It had been weeks earlier, but I had no trouble remembering.

So, after offering a handful of physical details — how many bunks in each barracks, the actually decent quality of the food, things like that — I turned to some of the people. After mentioning a few of my fellow inmates, I said, "And there was this guard."

Stoica perked up.

"Shinsky," I said. "Really fat. Disgustingly fat. Shinsky. We called him Shitpile."

"And the commandant?"

"Skinny little weasel. What was his name? Malakov? Yeah, Malakov. His nickname was Baby Shitpile."

With that, Stoica picked up a pencil and made two tick marks on the file. Shitpile. Baby Shitpile. Tick. Tick. At least, that's what I was hoping as I watched him.

He turned over the pages in the red file folder one more time. He turned them with his left hand and tapped on the desk pad with the eraser side of the pencil in his right hand. Turn, several taps, stop. Turn, several taps, stop.

Then Captain Stoica looked up and smiled.

"That's all for now," he said. He waved me toward the door and reopened the ledger book. He wasn't watching when I left.

"Open or closed?" I said.

He didn't answer. I left it open.

And whether or not Stoica intended it, the only two words that imprinted on my brain were the last two. For now.

38

My excursion to No. 5 Demetru I. Dobrescu had sobered me up most thoroughly, which meant that another trip to the English Bar was in order. I still had a whole night and half a day to kill before the visit to Constantin's cousin, the forger, and I knew myself well enough to understand that as my nervousness over Stoica and his red folder ebbed, my anticipation/terror about the mission to Jilava would build. Through every stage of ebbing and anticipating, alcohol seemed appropriate.

But when I walked into the lobby of the Athenee Palace, something was blocking my path toward the English Bar. Something, someone: Sofia Popescu.

"Jesus Christ," is what I muttered to myself when I saw her. First, my unnamed partner. Then, Stoica. Now, Sofia. If I had had a more eventful four hours, it wasn't recently. At least, I couldn't remember it.

She hugged me, then looked at me expectantly. I'd only learned about her husband about two hours earlier and really hadn't had a chance to process the news, given the Stoica interregnum and the persistent thoughts about electrodes attached to my balls. I didn't know exactly what to say, so I stalled for a minute in the time-honored fashion.

"Let's get a drink," I said. The look on her face when I said it was, well, not joyful. I realized that "Let's get a drink" was akin to the cops knocking on the door and saying, "Can we come inside?"

Radu didn't ask me what I wanted. He looked at Sofia and she said, "White wine, chilled." The look on his face was one of feeling insulted, as if he was the kind of bartender that didn't know to chill the white wine. In the two minutes it took for him to bring the drinks, neither of us said a word.

After my first sip, I said, "Here's the thing—"

"Oh, no..."

She was crying.

"No, no, your husband is alive. At least, that's the word I received from my contact."

"But why didn't you—"

"I just found out — it was only about two hours ago," I said.

Sofia wiped her eyes and sniffed up a ration of snot. She took her first sip and then said, "Well?"

"So, I do have some news," I said.

She said nothing.

"It's, um..."

"Is he injured?"

"No, no."

"Then, what?"

"It's just..."

I hesitated, and then I said, "I need a minute," and made like I was headed out to the lobby to use the toilet. Instead, I detoured up to my room and was back in five minutes. In that time, up the elevator and then down, I made the decision.

When I returned to the bar, I saw that Radu was refilling her wine glass.

"Here's the thing," I said. "Like I told you, I heard this from my contact just today. He said that your husband is not a prisoner in a labor camp in Ukraine."

"What? Of course he is. I saw them take him. If he's not a prisoner in Ukraine, then where is he?"

"He's in Ukraine and he's in a labor camp."

"What? What you're saying makes no sense."

"Let me finish. He's in Ukraine and he's in a labor camp — but he isn't a prisoner."

Sofia looked at me, open-mouthed.

"What?"

"He isn't a prisoner," I said. "He a Securitate agent. He's there on business."

"Securitate business?"

I nodded.

"That isn't possible," Sofia said. "My Mikhal, he's a farmer. And I love him more than anything, but he doesn't have the... the..."

She stopped, took a long drink.

"He isn't smart enough for that," she said. "I do the purchasing. I keep the books. He drives the tractor and whitewashes the fences."

"That's my information," I said.

"That he's Securitate?"

I nodded.

She sipped. And then I watched as she thought the whole thing through. It felt as if I was somehow prying as she took a dive down her own personal rabbit hole, but I couldn't look away. And gradually, over the course of a minute or two, I could see her talking herself into the possibility. I would have loved to have asked but I didn't want to interrupt the process. What was the trigger? A time when he sat with some unknown man on the front porch for a while, a man he said was a salesman? A phone call in the middle of the night that he went down to the kitchen to answer, insisting it was a wrong number when he returned to bed? But a five-minute wrong number?

I could only imagine. But I could see the look on her face turn and turn and turn again, from disbelief to bewilderment to, well, to maybe. And then, in the end, after emptying the wine glass a second time, she looked up and whispered, "Son of a bitch."

Then, she said, "So, what? I guess I just go home and wait for him."

"One possibility, certainly."

"Meaning what?"

"Meaning, I think we need to think about this for a minute," I said.

I reached into my breast pocket and took out the envelope I had retrieved from my room, the one containing $2,000.

"You said you have two children, right?"

Sofia nodded.

"Well, this will get the three of you out of the country."

"I can't leave the country."

"You might want to reconsider that."

"But the farm."

"Which is a financial disaster."

"It's all we have."

"From what you say, it isn't much."

"But why?"

"Because," I said, and then I explained what I had been thinking. It was a bit of a monologue, maybe two minutes in length. She listened, and then she acted as if she didn't understand. So, I repeated it. This time, I could tell that she heard me but I wasn't sure if the words had completely registered.

"Leave the country and escape to where?" Sofia said.

"Vienna. But does it really matter?"

"But I don't know anybody in Vienna."

"All the better," I said. There was no way I was going to tell her that she would know me if I ever got home.

"But, really, why?" she said. And so, I went at it a third time.

"The Securitate knows what I'm doing," I said. "They know about my list of names — not the specific names, not your husband's name, but they know about my list and that I'm trying to get these men of Ukraine, just like I got out. They know what I'm doing. They've questioned me twice. The first time, the captain from the Securitate was sitting on the same stool you're sitting on."

Sofia looked down and squirmed in her seat, just a little.

"If they know what I'm doing — and, like I said, they definitely know — they'll know soon enough about you searching for your husband," I said. "They'll know the names on my list. And, well, ask yourself. I don't know what your husband is doing, but it's important enough that my government contact — the guy helping me — is shitting himself. So, I can't imagine why the Securitate wants somebody in one of those camps, and you can't imagine, but if it's important enough that, when they find out his wife is trying to find him and spring him, well, who knows?"

"They'll think I am what I am, a loving wife worried about her husband," Sofia said.

"One possibility, certainly."

"But..."

"It's clear that they don't like the smell of me," I said. "They're watching me, and you've just met with me in a public place, and if my stink transfers to you, even just a little..."

We were both quiet for a few seconds. I thought about pressing harder but just fell back to the facts. I told her about the railroad yard and about the sealed boxcar to Vienna, and the 3 a.m. check-in requirement. Then I handed her the matchbook from Long Legs and told her that was the necessary identification. She looked at it and laughed.

"The first $1,000 for you is already paid," I said. "What's in the envelope is for the children."

The envelope was sitting on the bar in between us. She tapped it with her finger.

"Just fucking go," I said. "Just scoop up the kids and fucking go."

She didn't say if she would or she wouldn't, but Sofia did take the envelope and the matchbook. When we stood up, she hugged me, tight, and her right hand went exploring. When it found my pants pocket, she reached in and took out the room key. And then she, and the envelope full of money, and the key walked out of the English Bar, and down the half-flight of steps, slowly, slowly toward the elevator. I watched her, and I watched the doors close, and then I traced her steps across the lobby and to the elevator. And then I pressed the button.

39

Constantin and his cousin were waiting at the tea shop when Bogdan and I arrived. We were 10 minutes early, and they were earlier.

The vehicle was parked out front. It was something like an American jeep, beat-up but painted all black — war surplus of some sort, repurposed by someone for some reason. Whatever. It would do.

In the back, I could see two uniforms laid out. I assumed that the rifle and the pistol were hidden beneath them.

The tea was poured and the chit-chat was minimal. It was Constantin who said, "So what does the paper need to look like?"

I asked the cousin, whose name was not offered, what kind of official-looking letterhead he might be able to produce. He said that he had nothing that would pass even a cursory inspection.

"All right," I said. I was looking at Constantin. "The address of the Securitate headquarters—"

"No. 5 Demetru I. Dobrescu," he said.

"So it's well-known?"

"It is to me."

"And to a prison guard at Jilava?"

"Yeah, likely."

"Likely or very likely?"

"Very likely," Constantin said.

"Okay," I said. Then I directed the cousin to prepare a letter with the address at the top — the address and nothing else.

"On your best paper," I said.

The cousin looked at Constantin. He nodded. The cousin went into a back room.

"You saw the vehicle?" Constantin said.

I nodded.

"And the uniforms? The weapons are underneath."

I nodded again.

"I don't know..."

"Your part is almost over, as soon as your cousin brings the letter out," I said. "It's appreciated and it's over. Bogdan and I will take it from there."

"I know, but..."

"No buts."

"I feel it's my obligation. I feel responsible for you. You two, you're..."

"Again, it's appreciated," I said. "But the decision has been made."

His cousin returned in five minutes. The letterhead, with the address on top, was printed on gleaming white paper. It was well done, clean, no smudges. He also brought a second copy, on more ordinary paper.

"This might be more, I don't know, military — less fussy," he said.

"Yeah, but we want the best paper."

"Why?"

"It indicates a level of, I don't know, specialness," I said. "It will make up for the lack of a formal letterhead — well, not make up for but substitute for. The bright white paper says the same thing. Special. Important."

The cousin shrugged.

"You have a regular typewriter?"

He nodded.

"The typing doesn't have to be perfect. Here. It's only two sentences."

I handed him what I had written out beforehand, and he took it to the back room.

"So, when?" Constantin said.

"Now."

"Like, right now?"

"Like, immediately," I said. "It's Day 4, remember. We might be too late as it is."

"Probably too late."

"Maybe too late," Bogdan said. They were the first words he had spoken other than a muttered "thank you" for the tea, and there was a defiance in the tone that I liked. He had seemed to slip in and out of catatonia, and the last thing I needed was Bogdan in a funk. The last thing Florin needed.

The cousin brought back the letter requesting that Florin be released into the custody of the bearer for transfer to Securitate headquarters at No. 5 Demetru I. Dobrescu. I signed it with an indecipherable flourish and then asked the cousin if he had any kind of stamp with red ink that might make the whole thing look more official.

He went into the back room and brought out a cigar box containing various stamps along with a stamp pad. Most of them made no sense — they were things like PAID and OVERDUE that had to do with billing statements.

But there was one that had a chance:

URGENT

"Right next to the signature — maybe smudged a little, not too fussy, maybe overlap the signature just by a half-inch," I said. He complied, and I took the pen and scrawled some initials over the URGENT — different initials than the signature. It probably wouldn't matter, but a close inspection would indicate a second person being involved in the letter. And the story Bogdan told would measure up.

He would say, "All I know is, I was told to pick up the letter at one office, then sent upstairs to another office, and then the secretary took it back to somebody and returned it 30 seconds later with the big red URGENT on it."

Bogdan would be the one who had all of the lines. We had already gone over it three times, and we would do it twice more after we left the tea shop and drove the vehicle into a clearing that was maybe a half-mile from Jilava. The first mix-up: it was two pistols hidden beneath the uniforms, not a pistol for Bogdan and a rifle for me. And, well, whatever.

We were changing into our uniforms, and Bogdan — who had pissed once at the tea shop — was pissing again, not 20 minutes later.

"I'm fucking nervous," he said.

"You'll be fine."

"One more time."

"One more time," I said.

I would have loved to have been the one who went into the prison, leaving Bogdan in the vehicle outside, but my Romanian wasn't good enough. I might be able to bluff my way through a gruff-asshole kind of encounter, but anything requiring a conversation would give me away. It had to be Bogdan.

"What's the most important thing?" I said.

"Be a prick who doesn't give a shit," he said, with a little bit of the kind of sing-song that a child replies to his parents when they are asking a stupid question that had been answered a dozen times already. Brush your teeth. Take out the garbage. Be a prick who doesn't give a shit. The same, kind of.

"That's the whole game," I said. "Be a prick. Act like you don't give a shit because you don't. Any delay, any complication, and it's just like that: 'Fuck it — I get paid either way.' And if they want to call headquarters, or their boss?"

"Call, knock yourself out," Bogdan said, parroting back the script. "All I can tell you is the guy who signed this thing was fucking furious when he signed it. I thought he was going to rip the paper, he was so mad. And I have no idea about the guy with the URGENT stamp, but the secretary — a hot little number, by the way — looked a little scared. The scared part made her even hotter. But go ahead, call him. Like I said, I get paid either way."

"Good, good. And if the guy says he has to call his own boss and interrupt his dinner, say, 'Whatever. But what's your name? And what's his name? I'm going to need to tell my guy something if we're late.'"

Bogdan nodded. His hands were shaking so badly that he couldn't do the button on his tunic. I helped him and then said, "But I'll be damned if I'm doing up your fly."

He looked down. Only the top button was done.

"Fuck it," I said. "The coat will cover it."

40

Seeing as how we had not done any kind of reconnaissance at Jilava, everything was just a guess. But my thought was that the shift change of the guards — and, more importantly, the big bosses — was probably at 4 p.m. It seemed that 8-to-4, 4-to-12, and 12-to-8 was the likely schedule of shifts — and if 12-to-8 was obviously the sleepiest and safest way to go, it made no sense that the big suits at No. 5 Demetru I. Dobrescu would be working in the middle of the night, scrawling and stamping URGENT and whatnot. So, it had to be sometime after 4 — soon after, though, for big suits at Securitate headquarters reasons and another, more important reason. That is, it was Day 4 — and if Florin wasn't already gone, he soon would be.

I settled on 5 p.m. We were still parked in the clearing, and Bogdan was behind a tree, taking a shit this time. Christ. I had seen nervous people before — nervous before operations — but I'm not sure I had ever seen someone with such a big part to play unable to last 20 minutes between bathroom trips. But, well.

"Ready?" I said when he got back.

"Ready as I'll ever be."

"One more thing."

"If it goes..."

"Wrong," I said.

We had rehearsed that, too. If the guard on duty insisted on calling in his boss for a look at the paperwork, fine, fuck it, I get paid either way, et cetera. But if the boss insists on making a phone call to Securitate headquarters, well, all the attitude in the world wasn't likely to survive that.

"But, still, you wait," I said. "Don't give a shit. No skin off my nose. And then you have to play it by ear."

Bogdan looked at me, scared.

"No reason to shit yourself," I said. "We've been through all of this. You watch the boss on the phone. He asks you the name of the guy who signed it, and you say you don't know, and he can't read it. So, he talks on the phone, trying to get some kind of confirmation from somebody at Securitate. And you watch him. Hopefully, the bosses have left for the night there, too."

"And if they haven't?"

"You watch the guy on the phone," I said. "And if it looks the least bit like trouble, you say, 'Let me tell my partner in the vehicle that it's going to be a minute,' and you come out and we get the fuck out of there. And if he tells you not to go — like, orders you — then you start blasting away and then get out here, and I'll cover you from the door. But, only then."

"Only as a last resort."

"Only as a last resort," I said. "And one other thing."

He looked at me.

"Before they insist on making the phone call," I said. "You're all fine, fuck it, I get paid either way. But you also say, 'Well, can you at least check if the guy is here before we go calling one of the bosses away from his pre-dinner drink.' That's if they haven't checked their roster already. They probably will have, but make sure. And if Florin is gone, ask where. Like, 'Christ, they don't know which hand is wiping their ass sometimes. So where the hell is the guy now?' It's always like that, the tone. Cocky."

"Don't give a shit," Bogdan said.

"Right, right," I said. At which point, he stepped out of the vehicle. One more piss.

41

The guard in the shack at the opening of the chain-link fence could not have cared less. He looked at the paperwork for something just north of a nanosecond and waved us inside. He picked up a magazine as we drove away, a German magazine called *Bounce!* On the cover were three girls – blonde, naked from the waist up. They were running along the shoreline. Amazing what you can see in a split second sometimes.

The whole setup was relaxed — the guard and the fence itself, flimsy and without even a single strand of barbed wire along the top. There were five vehicles parked in front, and they all looked like personal cars. While I was parking, backing into one of more than a dozen empty spots, a public bus clattered by. At the main entrance, there was no guard outside. It was like a light bulb factory, or a soda bottling works, or any small plant you could imagine. Sleepy didn't begin to describe it.

I parked and handed Bogdan the letter. He pocketed it, and I guess my concern showed on my face.

"I'll be fine," he said.

"Of course you will."

"No choice but to be fine. No choice for Florin."

I nodded. He left. It was past twilight, and there was only a single bulb illuminating the entire parking area — one lamp over the main entrance to the prison, and not a particularly bright one at that. Standing under the light, Bogdan tried the door and it didn't budge. Some security, then. He pounded on the metal with the flat of his hand, once, twice, and stepped back. Somebody looked out of the peephole, and then Bogdan was allowed in.

I looked at my watch and tried to relax. Even if it all went perfectly, it would likely take 15 minutes for Florin to be retrieved from his cell and brought out to the guard in front. There was nothing for me to do but wait and worry about whether I had prepared Bogdan well enough.

I pulled the pistol out from the space behind the driver's seat and laid it in my lap. From where I had parked, I had a clear view of the big metal door out of the driver's side window, an unobstructed shot if I needed it. Part of me wanted to prop the pistol on the open window, but no. Not yet.

Five minutes. As the dozens of thoughts — worries, concerns — flew through my head in a repeating loop, for some reason, I allowed Fritz to enter the parade of worry. Fritz. What would he say if he knew I was risking everything on a long shot attempt to get Florin out of jail? I could argue that it was all part of my cover, entirely consistent with the character I had established, but, well, really? I could just hear the old man saying, "Ain't nothing worth getting dead over — especially a local." I could hear myself explaining to him that Florin was just a kid, and that his brother was a valuable asset, and I could hear Fritz saying, "I don't care what kind of kid he is. What part of 'not worth getting dead over' don't you understand?"

And, well, fuck Fritz.

Ten minutes. I moved the pistol closer to the window.

Bogdan and Florin, true believers. They weren't doing it for money — because, as best as I could tell, there wasn't any money. They were Romanian patriots, and they hated what their country had become under the Communists, and they were determined to do something about it. And if Florin was too young to do anything but follow his brother around, Bogdan, well, when I closed my eyes, I sometimes thought about what I had been like before the Nazis marched into Austria, what I had been like after they had marched into France. Because I had been that way, too, back then. I had been a true believer — or, well, at least not a cynical non-believer. It was hard for me to imagine sometimes, imagine what it felt like beneath the years of emotional callouses. But it had been there, I knew. There had been a desire to do right, to make a contribution. There had been a recognition of evil in my face, and there had been a determination to try to do something about it. What could one man do? If I didn't know the answer to the question, it didn't mean I wouldn't attempt an answer. Back then, I would try. Back before the callouses, I would take a stab at it.

Fifteen minutes.

Twenty.

Twenty-five. And then the big metal door swung open, and out came the two brothers, Bogdan and Florin. Out they came, Florin with his hands cuffed in front of him, Bogdan holding the pistol. Christ. It fucking worked.

I started the vehicle and laid the pistol back down in my lap. They were walking toward me, acting as if they didn't know each other. What must that have been like inside, in the moment that Florin was brought out from his cell? I hadn't prepared Bogdan for that instant, the one where the brothers' eyes locked, but it must have gone okay.

I was parked about midway back in the lot, maybe 100 feet from the metal door. Bogdan and Florin were out of the reach of the single light over the door, but I could see them well enough — and if they were mostly in silhouette, they weren't completely dark. I could still make out their features, especially as they got closer.

And then it happened. Two, three spotlights suddenly filled the parking lot. I was looking out the driver's window, and the lights were coming from behind me, from the passenger side — the side facing the street.

Bogdan and Florin froze in the bright lights.

I instinctively lifted the pistol from my lap.

The gunfire came in a rapid burst. It came from at least two machine pistols, I figured. It wasn't a calculation as much as it was a feeling, less a thought than an intuition. The shooting came from where the lights were, from the street side of the lot, maybe outside of the fence, maybe inside. I never looked back that way, though. I just looked at Bogdan and Florin — frozen in the lights and then cut down where they stood. I was fixated on Florin for some reason, and on his face — the way his eyes went wide when the spotlights hit him, and then the way his face contorted when the shooting started. He raised his hands, shackled together, as a kind of reflex, but it didn't matter. In the bright lights, I saw the left side of his head blown off as he fell. I saw the burst of red. I saw it at bedtime for weeks.

He was dead, and Bogdan was just as certainly dead, and I was next. That, too, was certain. And so I did what I could. I put the jeep into gear and floored it and headed for the front gate. I floored it, and I ducked down, and I fired the pistol wildly in an attempt to gain even a second or two of cover. And I hit someone. At least, I thought I hit someone, thought it because of the scream.

Did I? Didn't I? There was no way to know, not for sure. But I did get the pause, the briefest of pauses, maybe a second. As it turned out, it was all I needed because it got me to speed. But it was quick, so quick, and then the machine pistols shattered the glass and peppered the metal of my vehicle. The noise, the awful cacophony, it would haunt me like the picture of Florin in the days and weeks to come. Still, somehow, I managed to get away. I burst through the wide-open gate — past the guard and *Bounce!* — and nobody followed. There was just more gunfire as I sped down the road and into the night. More, and then less, and then just a few isolated pops, and then it stopped.

PART IV

42

The shooting came from outside the prison, not inside.
How?
Who?
It was all I could think about as I made my way back into Bucharest. I did not grieve for Bogdan and Florin — not then, anyway. In the moment, I had come to view death — death up close — as an observer with a freakish kind of detachment. When I thought about it, I thought about Leon and what he used to say about being a newspaper reporter. That is, "The job is to remember the color of a man's hair and the cut of his suit even though his face has been blown off by a shotgun."

I was a good reporter, then. I was a chronicler, a collector of facts and images and impressions. They were like snapshots that riffled past. The two of them walking out, Bogdan holding the pistol, Florin's wrists cuffed together in front of him. The spotlights suddenly bursting. The machine pistols. Bogdan and Florin falling. Again and again, the images flew by. The images and the questions.

How?

Who?

It took me close to two hours to walk back into the city after ditching the vehicle and the uniform. It was a good amount of time to think. I looked at my watch and knew that there would be time to collect the last of the money from the rooming house and head to the railroad yard for a 3 a.m. arrival — and if I didn't have the Long Legs matchbook, I could still describe it and there was still enough money to get myself hidden in a sealed boxcar to Vienna. It was the logical thing to do. I knew that in my head, and yet I managed to banish the thought. Or, at least, to shove it into a corner of my brain.

Because I needed to understand what had just happened. The whole sequence just didn't make any sense. I knew there were a half-dozen ways the plan could have gone to shit, but that hadn't been one of them. In all of my morbid imaginings — and I had a ton of them — I had never conjured up a picture of that scene. Not that kind of a massacre. Not from behind.

How?

Who?

I tried to play it out in my head. Bogdan goes in there and hands over the paperwork and puts on his I-don't-give-a-shit attitude. At that point, the guard either makes a call to instruct the guards to collect Florin from his cell or he calls in one of his superiors. Let's say it was the latter. The boss comes and looks over the paperwork, and he makes the next call — either to fetch Florin from his cell or to call Securitate headquarters. Fine. That had all been mapped out ahead of time.

Depending on what Bogdan sensed during the phone call to Securitate headquarters — assuming there was a call to Securitate headquarters — he was supposed to hang tight if things seemed normal or make his excuses about needing to tell his driver that it would be a few more minutes. Clearly, neither of those things happened. Instead, they brought Florin to him, and he put the cuffs on him, and he walked him out the door.

So where did the floodlights and the machine pistols come from?

Let's say Bogdan was stupid as to what was happening during the phone call. Let's say, given his nervousness, he couldn't read the room. Let's say the guy on the Securitate end of the conversation told the prison boss that the letter was bullshit and that they would be there in 10 or 15 minutes to take Bogdan into custody. In the meantime, they told the prison boss that he should just act like he's getting Florin's paperwork done before his release, and that Bogdan should take a seat and wait.

All of that was possible. We hadn't played it out that far ahead of time, but, well, it could have gone that way. In hindsight, it easily could have gone that way. But it still didn't explain the searchlights, and the machine pistols, and the massacre of Bogdan and Florin. If the Securitate was on to the scheme and wanted to sweat Bogdan and Florin to find out what they were all about, fine. Cutting them both in half with automatic pistol fire accomplished nothing but the creation of a gory spectacle. The Securitate, by all reckoning, was as bad as the Gestapo and the KGB and all of their other bastard children. But the truth was that none of them lived on death so much as on information. Or, rather, the death only came after the extraction of the information. Death was like the dessert.

And that was not this. This was different. This was an execution, dangerous and out in the open, not far from where a public bus ran. It was too much. There was no subtlety to it. It was out of character — not secret, not sinister, just brutal.

And there was another thing, too. Yes, I was pretty sure that I winged one of them as I sped through the gate. I heard the scream — or, at least, I was fairly sure I did. But even with that, why didn't they chase me? Maybe they were all out of their vehicles and thought I had enough of a full-speed head start to be uncatchable. Maybe. But not even to try?

There was so much I tried to process during that walk back into Bucharest. So much, with so little success. Two hours to walk, maybe three more hours to drink in three different bars, so little success.

43

I trudged into the rooming house, still unsure about what was next. I was likely headed to the rail yard, but if I was leaving, I wanted to scoop up the money and the radio hidden side-by-side between the mattress and the box spring. Even if it wasn't to be that night, I needed to be prepared.

I hadn't reached the staircase when Ion's door opened.

"A visitor," he said, pointing upstairs with his eyes.

I stopped.

"Female visitor," he said. But there was no dirty smile, no leer. When I opened the door to my room, Sabina was sitting on the edge of the bed. She looked frightened at first, at the sound of the knob turning, and then relieved. She stood up and hugged me, and I very much appreciated being hugged. Then we sat next to each other on the bed, and I waited.

"The Securitate," she said.

"What about them?"

"It's really your fault."

"What are you talking about?"

She stood up, walked across the room, and perched her ass on the window sill.

"Well? What?" I said.

Eyes down, Sabina said, "They came around, asking about you. And I... well..."

I closed my eyes and felt myself shaking my head. I muttered a "fuck," but that was about it. I felt like throwing up.

"Your fault, really," she said. It was barely audible. I looked up at her but she was fixated on the floor. Fuck.

"My fault?" I said.

"Your fault."

"How?"

"From what they said, they followed you after you left my place that night. What was I supposed to do? I didn't have much choice."

"Well, some choice," I said.

"Really, no choice," Sabina said. She wasn't crying but she also wasn't far away.

"What did they say? What did they want to know?"

"Two of them. Banged on the door, woke me up in the middle of the night. They knew your name and they wanted to know everything I knew about you."

"So they said, 'Who is this Alex Kovacs?' And you told them? What did you tell them?"

"That you're Austrian," she said. "And that I met you a few weeks ago in the café. And that I really didn't know much more than that — which is the truth."

"And the meetings in the back room?"

"Never came up."

"And you never brought it up?"

Sabina shook her head. And I felt two things at once: that I did believe her, and that she wouldn't lie about the meetings in the back room of The Dancing Waters if they asked.

I stood up and blocked her view while I reached beneath the mattress for the envelope. Sabina didn't need to know about the radio. I counted what was inside and realized there was more than I expected. There was enough to get her out, too.

"No," she said, again in a near whisper.

"But..."

"It's my home."

"But it's a fucking—"

"It's my home," she said. "This is who I am. I was a Jew who hid behind a fiction of paperwork to survive the Nazis. Now I'm talking to the Securitate to survive the Communists. This is what I do. I survive. I survive in Bucharest. It is what I know. It is how I live and it is how I will die."

She stopped, shuddered.

"In Bucharest," Sabina said.

We sat together on the bed again. I held her hand, and neither of us spoke. The woman had betrayed me, and I held her hand.

"How long am I safe? I said.

"I don't know what you mean by safe."

"I mean—"

"It's not like they confided in me. My instructions are to contact them if I see you again, and that's what I'm going to do."

She stopped.

"Starting with the next time," she said.

With that, she left without saying a word. I followed her down the stairs, watched her leave the apartment building, and knocked on Ion's door. He looked petrified. But I needed a place to sleep, and common sense dictated that, given everything Sabina had just told him about the Securitate and Alex Kovacs, it shouldn't be my room upstairs. At the same time, it shouldn't be at the Athenee Palace, either, seeing as how Captain Stoica was suddenly so interested in Alex Kramer. How long would it be before the left hand at the Securitate figured out what the right hand was doing — if they hadn't already?

"One night," I said, and Ion looked stricken.

"You have that room in the attic that's been empty the whole time I've been here, right?"

Ion's face betrayed nothing. I said nothing and just waited.

"One night — and then you're gone, gone out of my life," he said. "And if they find you up there, I'll say you broke in."

I thanked him. He was getting me the key when the door to the apartment began to open. I froze. The pistol was upstairs in my coat. The hinges whined, and a shaft of light from the moon entered first, entered before Sabina.

"I almost forgot," she said, and then she handed me a sealed envelope.

"She asked me, maybe two hours ago — it's the reason I came over," Sabina said. "Part of the reason."

And then, without another word, she was gone again. Once I got up to the attic, I opened the note and must have read it a dozen times, trying to decide what to do. There wasn't much there, just a few words, but still. When I woke up, and then sat up, the paper fluttered to the floor. I had fallen asleep with it lying on my chest.

44

Alex,

I left this with Sabina in the hope that you checked at the café. Word has reached me about what happened at Jilava, about the tragedy. We need to speak. I cannot overstate the urgency. Meet me in the morning at Bucur Obor at 11 a.m. It will be crowded, but it is better that way. Don't worry. Just go about your business and I will find you. Again, I need to stress the importance that we meet. It really is vital.

V

45

V. Valentina.

And it struck me as so stupidly funny that my initial impression of the whole thing was just how feminine her handwriting was, the bitch.

Bucur Obor was a huge outdoor market. I had walked by it once, and it was like a dozen other outdoor markets I had seen from Vienna to Istanbul — men and women selling their shit out of carts and little stalls, spices and vegetables and trinkets and crap. Yelling, laughing, haggling — the time I had happened by, it had been a heaving sea of all of that and it probably would be again. Valentina was right in that way. It was counterintuitive, but amid a crowd like that was the perfect place for us to have a meeting.

But, honestly: what would I be walking into?

And could I afford not to find out?

Valentina. Bogdan was sure that she had been sleeping with Constantin, and that opening her legs was her only talent — other than saying no. I still wasn't sure. I had seen plenty of business organizations where the boss was more a charismatic kind of leader than anything, places where the No. 2 held a sharp pencil in one hand and a hammer in the other. The leader dreamed big dreams, and the No. 2 identified what parts of the dreams were actually possible. It might have been the definition of the best business organizations, in fact, that kind of a partnership, that combination of big plans and hard-headed implementation. So, in that sense, Valentina as the No. 2 made perfect sense. The rest of it, what Bogdan felt, could be chalked up to sexism — I mean, even if she was a fucking bitch.

Given all of that, well, why was she contacting me now? What about Jilava had triggered her? And where was Constantin in all of this? Was he going to be at the meeting, too?

I looked at the note a dozen times, searching among the words and between the lines — especially between the lines — for some hint that Constantin would be part of our little get-together at Bucur Obor. But there was nothing there.

Meet me...

I will find you...

I need to stress...

This was going to be me and her if I showed up. I mean, I was kidding myself — I was this far in, and of course I was going to show up — but still. I had missed the 3 a.m. cutoff time at the rail yard, which meant I had a day to kill before the next one. I might as well spend it trying to figure out what happened — and Valentina was offering at least the hint of an answer, or maybe an informed suspicion, or something. I had to play it out. I really didn't feel as if I had another choice.

Bucur Obor was as I had seen it the first time, a cacophony of commerce — row after row of merchants, most with permanent stalls under a bit of cover, some just out in the open. I had no idea how it was going to work, so I just went about my version of window-shopping, but without the plate glass to offer a reflection of what might be following behind me. Every time I stopped at a stall, the owner was out of his seat, and complimenting the good taste I had shown when I looked at the wallet/scarf/wheel of cheese/whatever. The compliment was inevitably followed by the quotation of a price, followed by me recoiling, followed by an impassioned sales pitch, followed by me starting to walk away, followed by a lower price quote, followed by me continuing to walk away, followed by an epithet that was sometimes muttered and sometimes shouted. I couldn't believe how many times in 20 minutes that I had been told I would be fucking sorry, that the stall down the way was offering shit compared to this one.

It was at a stall where they sold spices, brightly colored mounds of whatever piled next to an antique-looking brass scale, when I felt a hand on my elbow. Valentina. She guided me past the proprietor, who had yet to leave his stool. They nodded at each other, and the two of us disappeared behind the beaded curtain and into the storage area. There was a teapot already steeping.

"You're unhurt?" she said.

"I thought you knew."

"I was pretty sure about you. I was very sure about Bogdan and Florin."

"Who told you?"

"Someone," Valentina said.

So, it was going to be like that. Bitch.

"The someone isn't important — well, not that someone," she said. She stopped for a second and poured the tea. We both sipped. It was tepid.

"Why am I here, Valentina?"

She sipped again.

"This isn't easy for me," she said.

"What isn't?"

"I think it was Constantin."

"You think what was Constantin?"

"I think he was the one who sent the killers," she said. "I think he's the one who got Bogdan and Florin killed."

"That doesn't seem—" I said, and she stopped me.

"I know, but—"

"But nothing. It makes no sense."

It really didn't make any sense. He was the leader of the group. He had recruited Bogdan and Florin — and Valentina, for that matter. He had coordinated with the Americans through Jake the asshole, which meant he was in coordination-once-removed with the Gehlen Org, too. The missions they had done together, just in my time, well, they had been meaningful if not exactly monumental. They had been successful, too — until the Telephone Palace.

"Listen, are you two—" I said.

"Are we what?"

"You know what I mean."

She looked down and muttered, "Fuck you." Then, after a few seconds, she said, "It's not how it started. You know, I knew Bogdan and Florin before I knew Constantin. We weren't a package, but I was ahead of them in school."

"How far ahead?"

"A few years. In our neighborhood, well, you knew about people. I knew about Bogdan, what he felt, what he believed. Winks, nods — you just know. Florin was just a baby, but Bogdan — I knew. The first time he showed up in the back room at The Dancing Waters, I wasn't surprised."

She stopped, relit the light under the metal teapot.

"It's been, I don't, more than two years now," she said. "There have been others, too. One caught. One killed. One just disappeared — he always seemed a bit of a flake. That jackass from your place who got killed near the border. Bogdan and Florin, though — over a year together. And somewhere during that time, Constantin and I, we..."

She stopped again, fiddling with the tea, pouring me a bit more. It was hotter.

"I don't know," she said. "You get close to somebody, you sense things and then you push them away as quickly as they pop up. It's just easier that way, you know? It's only when you look back."

46

"What are you saying, Valentina?"

"All right," she said. "This is when it hit me. It was after the Telephone Palace, after it all went to shit. Constantin, we met up afterward, and he told me what happened, and I took it all at face value. Jake the asshole. I got it. It seemed, well, logical. You knew Jake. Hell, I'm sure you could see it, too."

I debated whether or not it was time to tell Valentina the truth, to explain how Bogdan and I had watched the whole Telephone Palace thing go down. I decided, what the hell. She was knocked off her pins when I told her, and then I went through the discrepancies between the story Constantin told and what Bogdan and I had witnessed. Specifically, that Jake hadn't gone in like a wild man but with a deliberate 3-2-1 countdown. And that Peter hadn't been instructed by Constantin to withdraw but, instead, had just run away.

Valentina took all of that in for a second, and then she smiled softly.

"So you didn't catch it, either?" she said.

"Catch what?"

"You saw it and you didn't catch it?"

"What are you talking about?"

"Remember how it went — remember how you just described it," Valentina said. "Jake opens the door and gets slaughtered. Constantin's machine pistol jams. Peter runs away. Florin ducks behind the packing cases and begins firing at the door, cover fire. He waves for Constantin to make a run for it. So Jake is dead, Peter has run away, Constantin has run away. There's still shooting going on — coming out of the door at Florin, coming from Florin at the door. There's firing until Florin runs out of bullets. It's only after that the soldiers come up from behind Florin and capture him. Do I have it right?"

I thought about it, replayed the memory.

"Yeah, yeah," I said.

"So, if all of that is true, how does Constantin know that Florin has been captured? Why isn't he dead like Jake? Constantin is long gone. There was still shooting when he was running, and it's not like he came back. He would have said so, but he didn't. He didn't come back. So, how does he know? How does he know Florin's been captured?"

It made no sense but it made perfect sense. Valentina was right. How did he know? And if there was a leap between "how did he know?" on the one hand and killing Bogdan and Florin at Jilava on the other — and there was a leap — Valentina was right.

"But why?"

"I don't know the why," Valentina said. "I can't even begin to figure it — I can barely wrap my head around the rest of it. But it maybe helps explain why the whole thing at the Telephone Palace went to hell. It was Constantin's intel about the guards inside that got the whole thing started, remember — the intel that was so bloody wrong."

The more I thought about it, the more the tumblers began to

fall into place. Well, a little. Because the why still hung out there, the big question unanswered. But the who and the what, they began to fit. How did Constantin know about Florin being captured? There was no explanation. And, well, how did the shooting at Jilava come from the outside? The Securitate being tipped off with a phone call from inside the prison just didn't make sense. It had to be because somebody had been told ahead of time about our plan to spring Florin. And who knew? Me, Bogdan, Peter, Valentina and Constantin. Oh, and the forger cousin.

"The forger?" I said.

Valentina shook her head.

"Doesn't explain the Telephone Palace," she said.

I thought for a second.

"Peter?" I said.

She scoffed.

"Sometimes the simple explanation is the right explanation," Valentina said. "And there's another thing."

I looked at her.

"Constantin was out all night," she said.

"Is that unusual?"

"Unheard of, except during an operation."

"Never came back?"

She shook her head.

Part of me was kicking myself. I had never considered Constantin — like, not even for a second. Well, maybe for a second. But I banished the thought as quickly as it had entered my mind. It just didn't make any sense. The truth was, it still didn't make any sense. But there it was. The only consolation I felt was that it wasn't my fault that Bogdan and Florin were dead. It had been a good plan and it had been executed with righteous intentions. I could pin any ration of guilt on myself if the circumstances were right — and the drinking was copious

— but there wasn't any here. It really wasn't my fault that I hadn't figured out the bit about Constantin knowing that Florin had been captured. Not my fault, not Valentina's, not Bogdan's for that matter. None of us saw it, not until it was too late.

Which left us where?

I asked Valentina.

"All I know is, I can't stay here," she said.

"You have somewhere to go?"

She nodded.

"Away from Bucharest?"

Another nod.

"Away from Romania?"

With that, Valentina shrugged. And then she flicked at the corner of her right eye.

47

The days had grown shorter in my weeks in Bucharest and the nights cooler. I really noticed it that last time I walked up the path to the top of Metropolitan Hill. The little lights along the path blinked on and cast eerie series of shadows, and the breeze caused me to button my jacket. Reflexively, I patted two pockets after I was done with the buttons. The envelope in my inside breast pocket held the money that would get me out of Romania. The pistol in my right side pocket would be my bluff, seeing as how I had spent all of the bullets firing into the night as I sped out of the gate at Jilava.

I reached the summit and paused — the cathedral dominating to my left, the government buildings and the rest filling the vista to the center and right. On the breeze, hitting me in the face, I could hear the chanting coming from the little chapel. It was faint from several hundred feet away, but it did carry in the wind. Just a little, anyway.

The benches were empty as the service was still not concluded. We had no meeting scheduled, none that I knew of — and, besides, who was left? Only Constantin, Peter and me —

and I could have scared Peter off with a loud bark. I wouldn't even have needed the empty pistol.

I sat down and looked in through the open door. Constantin was there as always, there amid the group of men on their side of the chapel.

I wanted this to be Constantin and I. In my final hours in Bucharest, this conversation needed to be had. And if I was running a risk, it was a calculated risk. We were in a public place, and the loitering of the worshipers after the service would protect me. That was my calculation, anyway.

When the priest was done and the people began to stream out of the door, I saw Constantin before he saw me. I could tell the moment because his face lit up.

I stood when he arrived, and Constantin hugged me.

"Thank God," he said.

"So, have you heard?"

"Yes, yes, I've heard."

"And all you can say is, 'Thank God'?"

"It was always going to be a long shot," he said.

"But not until you started shooting," I said.

He looked around to see if any of the other churchgoers had heard, but no one was quite that close. He motioned for me to sit down on the bench, and I did. He sat at the other end.

"I don't know what you're talking about," he said.

"The fuck you don't."

He shrugged, turned his palms upward.

"I don't know what you're talking about."

"Well, then let me fucking tell you."

And I did just that. He folded his arms, and I laid it all out. His face betrayed almost nothing. The only time he winced, and it was only for a blink, was when I said the bit about it being impossible for him to know that Florin had been captured outside the

Telephone Palace and not killed on the spot. Then, for the final punctuation, I added the part about Valentina telling me that he had been out all night. There was no risk to her — she had been gone for hours, I was sure — but that part also connected. The reaction was not a wince, though, but a soft smile.

"Hell of a lay, Valentina — I could tell you stories that would keep you warm at night," Constantin said. And then he just muttered, "Valentina, Valentina, Valentina."

Eighty percent of the worshipers were gone now, all of them heading down toward the path that had brought me up the hill. There were six people left — two sitting on a bench about 30 feet away, four standing in a circle nearer to the entrance of the chapel. I still felt okay, relatively protected by even that small cluster of people. Besides, I had never seen Constantin carrying a weapon except on a mission, and a quick scan did not reveal any unnatural bulges in his pockets.

He looked up at me and smiled and said, "Fine. You got me. The two of you figured it out. Congratulations. A fat lot of good it will do you."

I pulled out the gun and rested it on my lap.

"Well, no need to get dramatic," he said.

"I can't believe I was so—"

"Wrong?" Constantin said. "Taken in? You made it out like you were a professional. Hah."

I raised the pistol but still hid it from the remaining churchgoers, keeping my crossed legs in between. Just then, the two people got up from the other bench and began heading for the path, leaving the final knot of four chatting by the chapel entrance.

Constantin laughed.

"Aren't you going to ask why?" he said.

"Not sure I'd trust the answer."

"God's honest truth. Nothing to hide here, not anymore. I'm Securitate. No rank — 'special agent.'

"Your people are bad enough, stupid enough — but the Americans, they fucking take the cake. They're so anti-Communist and they're so gullible. I mean, they're just blinded by the whole thing. What do they call it — Red Scare? What we figured out a long time ago was that the best way to keep an eye on them, and to control them — and to take their fucking money, and there is tons of it — was to pretend we were with them."

"You mean, the whole thing—"

"A total sham," Constantin said.

"But Bogdan, and—"

"No, they were legitimate — Bogdan and Florin and Valentina and a couple who became before them. True believers, sadly. But what better way to keep an eye on them, and to find out who their friends were? We start the group. We collect people. We do our little bits of bullshit sabotage. We have our meetings. And then we wait for the Americans to show up with a wheelbarrow full of cash to help us. Oh, and Jake the asshole is part of the package. And then, you Gehlen people show up. It's just a goddamned puppet show, and the Securitate is pulling all the strings."

The whole thing was stunning. The Americans had been totally played. They'd lost money, they'd lost people, and most importantly, they'd lost time. The Communists were that much more entrenched, and now the Americans were without a foothold in Romania.

"And my predecessor?" I said. "Killed at the border?"

"Not sure what he knew, but it seemed a risk to allow it to go on with him much longer."

"And Jake?"

"Bah. Too arrogant to bother with any self-examination. I could have played him forever. That limp dick Peter, too. There's still some hope there. There's still a chance for me to spin this in a way where—"

Constantin stopped when the group of four erupted in laughter and then began walking toward the path. We were alone now. He looked at his watch.

"The reason I have been so forthcoming is, well, partly because I actually like you. Partly. The rest of the reason will be clear to you in about 30 seconds. They're never late."

"They?"

"My Securitate contacts," he said. "I think you've met one of them, Captain Stoica. Alex Kovacs. Or it is Alex Kramer?"

I looked over Constantin's shoulder. I saw the headlights playing in the darkness before I heard the strain of the engine.

48

I pulled the trigger almost out of reflex. I didn't even aim very carefully. When the pistol clicked, Constantin laughed.

"I knew it," he said. And then he laughed again. And then, I stood up and took a big windmill swing and bashed him on the temple with the butt of the pistol. He was bleeding and stunned — not knocked out but not quite all there either.

I started to run, but the Securitate car had reached the top of the hill and there was no way for me to avoid running through the headlights.

A shot rang out.

Missed.

I tried to get out of the light, veering one way and then the other like an American football player on one of the newsreels. And I did get away from the headlights until I didn't.

A second shot.

Missed.

The car stopped, and someone seemed to yell out of the driver's side window. Stoica? Wasn't sure. The reply was from Constantin, though. One word I heard very clearly:

"Kovacs."

The interplay between the two of them took maybe two seconds, but it was a vital two seconds for me. I was running in the opposite direction from the main path that had brought me up the hill. Two seconds, and then the engine roared again. Two seconds after that, the headlights found me again — found me and actually helped me.

The steps.

Where were those fucking steps?

There they were, there in the flash of the headlights, the hidden steps down to the street where Constantin's cousin had his tea shop. The light caught them for a second but then lost them — but it was enough. I could see the top step and, even though it was dark, there was enough light from the occasional window of the bordering houses.

Narrow, just a few feet wide. Sixty-five steps, uneven concrete steps, down, down. I almost slipped once, but the metal railing saved me. Down, down. I was at the bottom before I heard the voices at the top. Voices, and then a torch flickered down the steps, but it didn't catch me. I was pretty sure of that because of what I heard the first voice from the car say. It was Stoica, definitely Stoica. And what he said was, "Fuck."

49

"One more bottle," Fritz said. He was smoked already but he also was buying, so.

The Hotel Bristol was on the Kärntner Ring, front and center. The rooms on one side looked down on the state opera. There's a suite upstairs where the Duke of Windsor used to take the Simpson woman — you know, before. The American Bar was on one side of the lobby and the Bristol Bar was on the other side, the one facing the opera. We were in the Bristol Bar because it was closest to the door when we entered and because the bartender said he had plenty of champagne on ice.

We were onto the third bottle, and Fritz was still as bubbly as the bubbly.

"You'll never understand," he said.

"People died, Fritz."

"The result was worth it."

"People fucking died," I said, and he refilled my glass.

When I got back from Bucharest, I debated what to tell Fritz about how it all went down. I had broken a half-dozen of his cardinal rules but, in the end, I decided to go with the truth. I told him everything, every bit of everything, except for the part where I slept with Sofia Popescu. All I told him about her was that I gave her the money to escape.

"I wonder," he said.

"I don't."

"You're not going to try to find her?"

"I am not," I said. "For all I know, she pocketed the money and is living happily ever after on her farm."

Everything else, though, I came clean — about Sabina, and about the whole prison thing at Jilava, and about Bogdan and Florin ending up dead, and about my final confrontation of Constantin. It was a long debrief, hours, and Fritz took notes. I had never seen him do that before. When I was done, he was clinical. He didn't chew me out. He said he needed to take this to Munich — to Gehlen himself — and that he would be back in a week.

And this was a week. And he insisted on the Bristol — I found out when I got there, because of the champagne. Because this was a celebration.

"I've never seen him that happy," Fritz said.

"Him? Gehlen?"

"Yeah, the old man."

"Who you might be older than."

"A minor point. I can't tell you how thrilled he was."

"You told him everything?"

"Hell, no," he said. "But I told him enough. I told him the important part at the end. I told him that the Securitate has been fucking with the Americans for months and years. Man, he loved that. Just shoveling money to them, and essentially working for them without a clue. And what did he keep calling them? 'Those rich, arrogant assholes.'"

"So, what's he going to do?"

"Nothing for now. He's just going to sit on it, at least for a little bit. They still have their man in there, Peter—"

"The limpest dick that Uncle Sam ever birthed," I said.

"Yeah, I told him. He's going to wait and see what Peter reports back. As far as they know, you got sick and had to come home, and we don't have a ready replacement. We'll just see for a bit what happens — but Gehlen will spring it on them soon enough. What did he say? 'Those jerks need some embarrassing, and I'm just the one to embarrass them.'"

Leon walked in. I had told him to give us two hours, and he gave us exactly two. Fritz was getting up to leave, shucking on his coat. When he saw Leon, he grabbed the waiter and handed him a wad of bills and said, "One more bottle." He clapped Leon on the shoulder and kept walking.

"He's a happy old fuck, isn't he?" Leon said.

"You could say so."

"What, does he have a promise? That where he's headed?"

"Everything isn't about sex."

"If you say so," he said.

I explained the reason for the smile on Fritz's face. I had already given Leon the highlights/lowlights of the trip. He couldn't believe that I tried to pull off the same prison bit that we had pulled off together in Limoges — and that it had worked. Well, until.

"So, what do you figure?" he said.

"What do you mean?"

"I mean, I'm all for fucking with the Americans. But how long until Gehlen sticks it up their ass?"

"My guess is soon," I said. "I mean, put it this way: as soon as Gehlen can find a way to leverage it for more money. Because that's all this is about — money to establish the Gehlen Org, to give it roots, to build out the infrastructure, to put together something that will last."

"What are you, a business consultant now?"

"Think about it. West Germany — I mean, at some point it's going to be a country again, right? And countries need, well, they need Gehlens. And if he's already established and in place…"

I left the thought hanging. Leon whistled. We drank a toast to Bogdan and Florin. I had him rolling when I told him the story about Bogdan and the farting championship trophy. After a while, he got around to the question that he always got around to in the end.

"Women?" he said.

"Two," I said, and he pulled his chair a little closer and refilled the glasses from the fresh bottle.

ENJOY THIS BOOK? YOU CAN REALLY HELP ME OUT.

The truth is that, even as an author who has sold more than 250,000 books, it can be hard to get readers' attention. But if you have read this far, I have yours – and I could use a favor.

Reviews from people who liked this book go a long way toward convincing future readers of its worth. It won't take five minutes of your time, but it would mean a lot to me. Long or short, it doesn't matter.

Thanks!

I hope you enjoyed *Bucharest Unbound,* the 12th installment in the Alex Kovacs thriller series. I have also written books in two other series. One begins with *A Death in East Berlin* and features a protagonist named Peter Ritter, a young murder detective in East Berlin at the time of the building of the Berlin Wall. The other is the story of a Paris mob family in the late 1950s, beginning with *Conquest.*

That book, as well as the rest of all three series, is available for purchase now. You can find the links to all of my books at https://www.amazon.com/author/richardwake.

Thanks for your interest!

Made in the USA
Middletown, DE
01 April 2024